The Journey

Nicola C. Stokes

Cover image:
Copyright © Pilgrim's Path by Kev Pearson Photography

Printed in Australia
First Printing, 2016
ISBN: 978-0-9945052-5-5

White Light Publishing House
6 Lincoln Way
Melton West, VIC, Australia 3337
www.whitelightpublishingau.com

Dedication

This book is dedicated to my husband, David.

My traveller of realms, my soul connection,

my love, my forever.

I am a wanderer

the gypsy of my soul.

I journey through this lifetime

as I gather the knowledge

to become free and spiritually whole.

It is these gifts

I will carry with me

that will lead me to the end.

The end to which I travel

that will come around again

and again.

Nicola C. Stokes

Acknowledgments

I would like to acknowledge my wonderful friends for their encouragement and support.

My parents who though no longer here, are a constant guiding light. My mother Palma for her love and being my Spirit Messenger of Air. My father Russell for working so hard to get the message to me, to complete this book.

My son Ethan, my bright shining star. Thank you for choosing me in this lifetime to be your mother, I am so blessed. I love you so much.

Finally, to my love David. My confidant, soul mate, my past, present and future. For you're never ending love and support. I am forever grateful.

I love you all x

CHAPTER ONE

"Excuse me, excuse me", Ruby called out to the driver as she was running towards the furthest bus in the station. Panting as she neared the bus she adjusted her tilting backpack and bags. "Is this bus going towards Tintagel?" she asked the portly bus driver standing at the door. "Sure is young lady" he replied. "Phew", sighed Ruby with relief and exhaustion as she climbed the steps into the coach. "Mmmm, blue velour seats, just divine!" she thought to herself. She squeezed herself and her backpack down the aisle past the first four rows and chose a seat on the left behind the driver's side.

"Empty! Woo hoo!" she muttered to herself. With her seat chosen, Ruby swung herself into the window seat and put her backpack next to her on the empty aisle seat, secretly hoping it would deter anyone from wanting to sit there. It would be a long four-and-a-half-hour bus trip. She was so tired and exhausted from her flight and she knew it wouldn't be long before she was nodding off. "Bliss!" she thought., "It doesn't matter where I end up, so long as no one wakes me".

As the other passengers settled into their seats, Ruby felt that she could finally relax for a while. She had finally arrived after a long flight and the joy of thinking about no more plane food, cramped legs and stale air brought a smile to her face. She had to laugh to herself as now she was sitting in another tin can; this time with wheels, but oh so comfy and with the luxury of blue velour seats!

Unzipping the side of her backpack, she pulled out her travel pillow, propped it up against the window of the bus and laid her head against it. As she looked out the window at people in the station busily going about their day, she thought back to her recent bus trip in Morocco. Crazy! Yet such a wonderful adventure! Ruby loved adventure; she was always searching for the next one. "I suppose it was luxurious to have glass windows and blue velour seats", she chuckled to herself, thinking back to her bus in Morocco that had been much less comfortable. It had several windows missing, chickens running freely up and down the aisle, and she was concerned about her precious backpack being strapped with other luggage onto the bus roof. Her concerns had been warranted when three hours into her trip along unmade bumpy roads, several boxes and some luggage had come unstrapped and fallen off the bus roof onto the dusty road. She remembered watching them tumble and all she could see was dust and hear chickens squawking in the aisle. She had quietly prayed one of them wasn't her backpack as the driver sped hastily into the mountains, oblivious to any loss.

All she had done to keep herself sane until she reached Fez was listen to her iPod as she shelled and ate her fresh peanuts she had bought in Tangier at the bustling medina marketplace before she had boarded the bus. She had left Australia looking for something. Adventure? "Well", she thought, "this was it!" Ruby wasn't so sure at the time. Looking back what a crazy time that had been. Rain started pitter pattering on the bus window, and it brought her back to the bus she was on with the oh so comfy blue velour seats and yes, with sealed glass windows!

She looked ahead over the seats in front of her and then backwards to the rear of the bus, "No chickens here!" she thought to herself. Unzipping her pack for her iPod she noticed her hands; she had forgotten about her beautiful hands. In fact, as she looked and gasped, they made her stop in her tracks each time she looked at them in detail.

Ruby loved art, she loved creating and painting, but now she was admiring her own hands that had become a masterpiece. She studied her hands as she held them in front of her. From the tops of her fingertips all the way to her wrists, were the most beautiful intricate patterns and designs. She followed the lines and spirals on her hands with her eyes, thinking of the day she had walked past a small stall in the medina of Souk El Arba; the destination of her crazy chicken bus trip. She had walked past a small stall in the medina surrounded by people selling their wares to the locals, when a woman had bid her to sit and have a drink.

The scorching Moroccan sun had made Ruby hot and thirsty. She was pleased with the offer, so she could shade herself from the intense heat for a moment. The market place was buzzing with incense, colour, noise, donkeys, vibrant fabrics, woven rugs, silverware and jewelry; a delightful overload for Ruby's senses. As Ruby sat, the woman smiled at her and passed her a beautiful red etched glass filled with peppermint tea, poured from a freshly brewed teapot. "Divine," thought Ruby as she bought the glass to her lips; the tea's fragrance immediately filling her nostrils and bringing her an immediate sense of relaxation.

As Ruby returned the glass of tea to the table, the woman took Ruby's glass from her hand, put it down on the table and began turning Ruby's palm facing upwards, then turning it back again as a palm reader would do. She held her hand out, gesturing to look at Ruby's other hand and Ruby obliged, not understanding what was happening but very intrigued. Ruby was imagining she was about to have her fortune read. She loved things like that, and was slightly surprised when the lady began to bring out a bowl of henna. "Oh well. When in Morocco, do as they do" she thought to herself. Ruby was up for anything.

As the woman began her art work with her cone tipped ochre paste, Ruby was mesmerized by how intricate the patterns were; the swirls, dots and all of them seeming to flow together into one as if unbroken. Ruby was very relaxed and had felt as if she had been sitting for hours as she was sure she would doze off and had felt a little dizzy and disorientated, but realised she still was yet to drink her tea.

Ruby looked into the woman's face as she was focusing. She thought she may be about sixty years old, yet such beautiful skin and long dark hair that was coiled up under her scarf. "What did she look like with her hair free? Beautiful, I imagine", thought Ruby. She had such exotic brown eyes, decorated with black kohl. They were so different from Ruby's green eyes and her fiery auburn hair with unruly wild ringlets.

The result of the henna work was nothing short of amazing. Never had Ruby seen such beautiful work; all spirals and lines connecting as if it told a story. Where did it begin, and where did it end? And why didn't she want payment? She was so kind. Ruby had felt honoured; humbled to be wearing such a beautiful work of art on her skin. As she stood up the woman had told her it was a gift of good fortune and happiness and she must follow the lines as she does her heart. Not understanding what she meant, Ruby thanked her and left in awe.

Jolting Ruby back to reality, the bus was just over half full when the doors closed and the engine started, and it slowly began making its way out of the station. The sky was now full of grey clouds; all joining to form one continuous cloud, covering the sky. "Funny how the weather affects your moods", thought Ruby. It wasn't long ago that she had been flying high above these very clouds, looking at a magnificent blue sky. The sun had been beaming its gorgeous rays into her little window and reflecting on the white, cotton-like clouds. Ruby was brought back to reality again from her little daydream as the first big drops of rain began to hit the bus window. And down it came!

iPod, where did I put my iPod? Ah yes! Ruby found it in the front zipper as she put her earplugs in. Settling back into her pillow, she watched the rain hit the window and followed the drops as they made their way down the glass; each one seeking its own pathway; some connecting with each other and others just happy to be alone.

She was warm, she was safe, and she was feeling very tired. Ruby felt her eyelids becoming heavy as she watched the outskirts of London turn into lush green countryside. Listening to Eva Cassidy on her iPod, she allowed herself to drift into a deep sleep.

CHAPTER TWO

Woken by a sudden jolt, Ruby felt very disorientated and wasn't quite sure where she was. She knew she was not at home in her bed, so became alert and quickly took in her surroundings; something which as a backpacker, she had become very familiar with. "Blue velour, oh yes! Bus... I'm in the bus", she said to herself. It was now dark outside and still raining, but not as heavy as when they had left London. What time is it? And how long have I been asleep?

Suddenly her deep peaceful sleep turned into slight panic, wondering whether she had she missed her stop. Where were they? Surely the driver would have woken me up? Pushing her wild auburn hair back over her ears and out of her eyes, she stood up and peered over the seat in front of her. She could hear the other passengers talking amongst themselves. Ruby looked outside to the front of the bus and could see the driver. She could see him in the headlights at the front of the bus on his phone, and he was getting very wet.

Outside all around the bus was darkness; it was pitch black. There were no lights to be seen in the distance, no house lights, and no cars; just darkness. Ruby sat back in her seat. She suddenly felt cold and weary, and a feeling of anxiety set in. She didn't like the feeling of something disrupting her trip; especially the unknown. It had always caused Ruby a feeling of uncertainty. She wasn't sure she liked uncertainty. She sat there telling herself that everything was going to be okay, and that they'd be on their way soon.

"Excuse me ladies and gents", the driver called out from the front step. He spoke loudly so all could hear. His voice was booming in Ruby's head as she was still feeling quite groggy from a heavy sleep. "We have had a slight change of plan. Sorry folks, but we have had a mechanical problem and it is too unsafe to continue". With that, all the passengers let out a communal sigh, but before anyone could talk, the driver continued in his big booming voice. "OK folks, it is late, dark and wet outside, so I have called up for backup for a local coach to take you to the nearest town until my roadside assistance arrives. It appears to be a major job. I appreciate this wasn't on your plans folks, but it looks like you must stay overnight. It's too late for transportation. The coach should be arriving within twenty minutes to take you. Best we can do, folks" he said as he stepped back outside into the front headlights.

The bus suddenly erupted with voices getting louder - some raising their voices, others too tired to care - they just wanted warmth and a destination. Ruby sat back in her plush blue velour seat and concluded, "Well, there's not much I can do but wait".

Stepping down from the bus, the rain had subsided, thank goodness. She looked at the driver who was still standing at the front door and was lit up by the headlights; his clothes saturated. She had felt when looking at him, that he was in for a long night; much longer than hers. She smiled at him, said "Thankyou" and turned to board the small bus behind. It was a small bus- only about a twenty-seater - so she shuffled along the aisle past all her travelers and smiled wearily at them hoping to offer a small piece of hope for the night. Some travelers were not too happy. She had resigned her weary body and mind that this must be part of her next bus memory. "The one that broke down on a wet dark night in the middle of nowhere", she smiled to herself. Maybe she should write a book about all her bus adventures; they certainly did give her something to think about.

As the small bus drove off, she looked out of the back window to see the driver still waiting alone in what seemed complete darkness, except for his headlights. The headlights got smaller and smaller until they disappeared, leaving Ruby looking up into the night sky which had cleared a little to reveal a few stars. She turned around and looked down the aisle of the bus as they sped off down the motorway – but to where?

Lamps and houses came into view. Civilization at last! As they wound through the streets, the sweet little homes looked so inviting with their welcoming lights and lamps on in the windows. It made Ruby just want to go to bed and sleep. As they neared the town centre, the driver spoke out that they had arrived in Glastonbury. All Ruby could wonder was how far Tintagel was from Glastonbury. Where is Glastonbury, and where will I stay?

That was soon sorted out as the driver was most helpful offering advice for accommodation. He had then arranged to meet back here in the town centre near The Abbey to be picked up for the continuing trip on the coach the next morning at 10am. Ruby looked around her and watched several groups of passengers chatting as they walked off to their chosen accommodation; each one saying goodnight to the others. She had an urge just to take a walk along the street to stretch her legs and decided she would join the group shortly.

As she walked with her pack on her back, she loved the street scape, the shops, the narrow streets, and the beautiful Abbey which she had initially walked past and kept walking, until she saw a sign that grabbed her eye saying, "Accommodation Available". It was on an iron post gently swinging in the cool night breeze with rain drops dripping from it as it gently swung back and forth. She looked towards the house and was delighted to see a quaint cottage aptly named Moonstone Cottage. This was a definite sign and it sparked Ruby up as she loved Moonstone; it was her favorite crystal.

"This is the one", she thought. As she approached the cottage, there was a bell. She rang it and waited. The lamps were on in the front room, so she waited a while longer until a front porch light came on and a lady opened the door. Ruby explained her situation and was welcomed warmly into the cottage. The open fire was crackling, breakfast was laid upon the kitchen table and the lady departed to the cottage next door, wishing her a good night's sleep.

Ruby scanned the room she was standing in. It was small, cozy and warm with paned windows at the front looking out to the road. The lamp sat in the window like a beacon. She put her heavy pack and bag down and finally stretched her arms out in the air, releasing all the tension from the weight of the bag and the bizarre night it had turned out to be. She went into the tiny kitchen with wooden benchtops and put the kettle on for a lovely warm cup of herbal tea. How lovely! The lady had left a selection of cheeses, biscuits and fruit to nibble on. It was so appreciated. Ruby hadn't eaten for quite a while and enjoyed the beautiful fresh foods.

Up the stairs were two small bedrooms and a bathroom complete with a deep bath, which looked so inviting to Ruby. She put the plug in and began running the hot water. As the bath was filling, she looked into both bedrooms and chose the front room with its window facing the street. The bed looked like a giant marshmallow and as she flopped onto the bed she sunk into the beautiful pillow surrounds. She could have nodded off straight away but the sound of the water running suddenly bought her back to reality. After a long soak in the deep bathtub, soaking out the day's trials and tribulations, Ruby changed into her cotton night dress and set her alarm to meet the bus in the morning. She turned down the sheets and jumped into bed.

"Oh my goodness", she said to herself, "This is bliss!" She leant over to turn the bedside lamp off. As she lay in the dark, she felt the warmth of the bath that had seeped into her bones and the soft fresh fragrant sheets that surrounded her. She felt clean and warm, and with heavy eyelids, closed her eyes to sleep.

CHAPTER THREE

"Why can't I sleep?" Ruby wondered as she pulled the covers off the bed. She sat up in bed, rubbed her eyes, swung her body out of bed and felt her feet touch the cool wooden floorboards. She slid gently off the bed and walked across the room to the front tiny paned window. It had been the light shining through the partly drawn curtains that had been keeping her awake. As Ruby began to draw the curtain with her right hand, she saw the beautiful henna designs illuminated on her hand, but she was instantly taken with the radiant glow of the moon in the night sky. It was a full moon; so high, so majestic. It seemed to be illuminating everything its beautiful light touched. It lit up the ancient Tor, the hill in the distance like a giant beacon. It intrigued her. Hypnotised for a moment, she found herself having to refocus her eyes, but was once again drawn to bathe in the moons brilliant glow.

Seeking adventure had always been Ruby's forte but as she found herself closing the gate latch behind her and making her way through the cobbled laneways lit by an odd lamp here and there, she had a fleeting thought: "What am I doing?"

She was guided by the moon light and the hill she had seen from her bedroom window. She had made it to the field, and through an old wooden gate; the path ahead now lit up before her as if the heavens were shining their lights down for her to follow. Ruby followed the pathway. It wasn't raining any more but the grass was damp with dew. She could feel the coolness beneath her feet and the night air was cool on her skin through her night dress. She continued to look up, feeling hypnotized and drawn by the radiant glow of this brilliant moon leading her up the terraced pathway to the crest of the hill. She was now standing at the hill she had seen from her bedroom window. Ruby had never felt so curious, so intrigued or drawn to explore, and could not turn back or ignore the beacon of light that was calling to her.

Approaching the rise in the hill, the pathway ended and it now became a grassy knoll and had levelled off. Ruby turned around and as she neared the summit, she turned to look back at the pathway she had just walked up. It had taken her some time; she looked back into the darkness as if she was on another planet looking back at Earth. She looked back down into the darkness of the village so far below; the street lamps now like a sea of stars so far away.

As she turned back towards the Tor; towards the light, she found herself looking up, following the Tor's ancient structure; from base to top of the tower, beautifully silhouetted by the massive full moon. Was that faint music she could hear? Surely not; it must be the wind playing tricks, so sweet and beautiful. She closed her eyes and drank in the sounds of the world at night.

Ruby opened her eyes slowly; half expecting to wake up in her soft bed back in the village, but something deep within her knew this was not so. When she opened her eyes, it was like no music she had ever heard before; soft chimes that were harp-like and hauntingly beautiful. She wondered if she had imagined it; so faint, so soft and yet so exquisite. The sound drew her gently to its source.

As she neared the base of the ancient Tor, the moon seemed so much brighter, it dazzled her eyes. She looked and then had to look away in to the darkness below to regain her balance. She looked once again and the moon now seemed to be acting as if it were a giant beam imprinting the earth below; creating a glowing labyrinth on the dewy grass.

As Ruby neared the glow upon the grass, she was guided to the opening of the labyrinth. She entered the labyrinth imprinted before her on the earth and slowly followed its pathway; winding around and inwards, journeying towards the centre. As she neared the centre, the path was clearer, the light more focused; so much whiter, brighter and more intense.

The music she'd heard had become louder as she spiraled into the centre; each turn taking her closer to the sound. The music became stronger and so beautifully filled her body with heightened senses. The earth beneath her feet began to hum; the breeze against her skin blowing. She looked down and the ground began to form a beautiful visual whirlpool of bright white light around her as if protecting her and gently drawing her down; cocooning her as the Earth beneath began to open around her; filling her with nothing but light.

Ruby was not frightened; she was aware that she was feeling this amazing energy surging through every cell in her body. As she let go and released herself to it, she released body and mind to the energy. She looked up for the last time and saw the clear dark sky with its diamond like stars above in the night slowly disappear. Silhouetted by the backdrop of the Tor and the glow of the majestic moon, Ruby knew she had been called.

CHAPTER FOUR

Ruby awakened to the gentle lapping sounds of waves, as she sat up slowly and regained her balance. Looking around her, she took in the scene before her eyes. She noticed the night sky so dark; lit by thousands of jewel-like stars, glistening upon the water; the heavens looked alight. She sat in awe of the sight above her and the largest moon she had ever seen sitting on the horizon. It illuminated the tip of the waves as they broke upon the shore. The waves looked like they were silver orbs twisting and playing, chasing one another as they gently crashed upon the sand. She looked down to where she was sitting upon the sand; so soft and golden under the moons brilliance. She stood; a little giddy at first, but as she rose and turned to her left, for as far as her eye could see, there were golden sands with waves lapping in to meet them. To her right, she also saw the sands but in the distance, there was an outcrop of rocks jutting into the water; the moon also lighting up the tip of the rocks as they were glistening like glass. Behind her in the shadows were darkened palms, swaying in the night breeze.

Ruby was overwhelmed and confused. "Where am I?" she wondered. She chose to make her way easterly along the shore line, to reach the outcrop as it glistened in the night. With her feet in the warm ocean waters, feeling the firm sand underneath, she enjoyed walking ankle deep along the shore, basking in the moon light.

As she approached the outcrop she realised it seemed so much larger now that she had gotten closer. The largest stone was twice her height and three times as wide. It reminded her of quartz. She had always loved clear quartz and its brilliance, and its ability to bring her infinite possibilities; her heart's desire. She had always worn a clear quartz crystal around her neck for this very reason. Ruby reached up and held the crystal around her neck as if for protection and guidance.

She felt the pull of the large rocks and their energy reaching out to her; she needed to touch the rock - to feel its power - but was hesitant. Had she manifested this dream? Was it a dream? It felt so real! She moved her feet in the water; digging her toes deep into the wet sand. Yes! It feels so real. Ruby gently placed her right hand up to the rock, and with her left, held her crystal amulet around her neck. She closed her eyes and expected it all to disappear. Opening her eyes, she took a step back into the water. Where she had held her hand, the rock had begun to change into a different form, as if it were becoming clearer. It was changing in front of her. Ruby couldn't believe her eyes. She closed and reopened them. Yes, it was transforming where she had touched it; it was becoming clearer only in that section. She placed her hand upon it again, in the same place. This time she not only noticed the rock changing, but her hand! Her hand was glowing; the markings on her hand were glowing!

She watched as the henna design began to glow and light up as if someone were drawing the designs on with silvery ink. The pattern was glowing in the darkness against the rock. As she connected to the rock, she felt warmth run through her body all the way to her fingertips. She watched the glow and the design become alive; illuminating as if someone were drawing a map. It wasn't until it had all lit up that something incredible happened. The rock underneath her hand became crystal clear. Ruby took her hand away, still feeling the warmth running through her body. She looked at her hand and the design had disappeared; all except a spiral like symbol with three dots along the side. These remained alight and glowed silvery upon her skin. She looked up at the rock where it had changed form and felt faint with what she saw. She pulled away from the rock, stepping aside from the mirror image. Ruby felt frantic. Where am I? Who am I? What's happening?

"Is that me?" she wondered. Ruby touched the rock again, and it had become so clear that it was like a mirror reflection. In fact, it *was* a reflection. She could see the moon glowing on the horizon behind her. Ruby was looking at herself in the rock face, but it wasn't her. "I look different; so different.

What's happening?" she wondered, as she began to feel a wave of panic. As she spoke into the rock, she could see herself talking and the image she saw was speaking at the same time. "It is me!" She took a deep breath, grounded herself and looked back at her hand. Everything had gone except the spiral symbol. She looked at the rock once again. She definitely looked different.

Ruby's hair was long and silken and straight. It was the color of the golden sands she was standing upon. She lifted her hand to her hair as she watched her reflection in the rock. She glided her hand from the top of her head, down to her shoulders and then gently pulled the long locks over her shoulder. Ruby looked at her hair in front of her. It was golden, silken and beautiful - something she had always wanted - unlike her wild crazy auburn ringlets. She suddenly felt overwhelmed; she suddenly missed her wild crazy auburn ringlets. Where were they? Where was she?

As beautiful as everything seemed, Ruby felt so alone. She turned from the rock and found a place to sit on the sand beside the outcrop and leant heavily against the rocks. She put her hands around her legs, buried her head and began to cry. Ruby cried silently, begging "Wake up, wake up, wake up".

How long had she been floating in this blissful state of dreamlike warmth and serenity? Ruby came to as she felt another's fingers stroking her forehead gently. For a moment, she believed she was a child again, lying in her bed with her mother stroking her face tenderly, feeling such comfort, reassurance and heartfelt love. She desperately missed her beautiful mother; taken away from her much too early by a sudden illness. The comfort began to feel like a deep sadness; an aching deep within her soul, filling her with a longing to reach out, to see, to hold her mother one last time. She felt tears slowly welling up and filling her closed eyes. The tears began to fall down her cheeks, as if so heavy from her sorrow. They fell to the ground that she lay upon.

It was when she opened her eyes that she found herself gazing into the most exquisite eyes she had ever seen. They were the color of amethyst, and like deep gemstone pools; as if scanning her as she stared into them. The face above her was the face of a petite featured, elven like young woman with unblemished pale skin, and long dark silken flowing hair over her shoulders. She was beautiful. "You must come with me. Please come with me", she said.

Ruby sat trying to take in her surroundings. She was unaware of the time that had passed, where she was, and how she had gotten there. She was very confused. Her mind was trying to retrace what had happened up until this point. She slowly sat up and looked around. No ocean. No golden sands. She felt like Alice in Wonderland just shortly after falling into the hole. She was so confused, yet intrigued at the same time. As she put her hands to the ground to help herself up she recalled her hand and how it had been glowing against the crystal rock. "Yes! My hand!" she thought as she looked immediately at it.

Ruby remembered the beautiful crystal outcrop and her spiral glowing design. She studied her hand and was surprised to see that most of her hand design had all but disappeared. All that remained was a small spiral that led into a larger spiral, and three small dots. "How curious", she smiled, envisioning herself as Alice. It was not glowing now at all, but in fact, looked like a marking, like a tattoo.

She looked up realising she was being watched by the beautiful young woman; those deep amethyst eyes twinkling at her. Ruby straightened herself up and as she stood she could not help noticing herself. She was different! Yes, she felt so different. She stood and stretched out as if she had been asleep for a very long time, not unlike a cat stretching every limb. She felt strong, taller and more feminine in her shape. She looked down at her body. It had definitely changed, she recalled her hair golden in the moonlight and reached to pull her hair over her shoulders. It was flaxen, silky and long over her shoulders and down to her hips. What had happened? She did not understand but whatever it was, she had to admit, she felt so good.

"Where am I? Who are you?" she asked the young woman in front of her. "My name is Maha, meaning Child of the Earth. Please, you must follow me. You are safe." Ruby looked at Maha. She was breathtakingly beautiful; her long dark hair flowing around her with every move she made. She was clothed in what looked like a robe made from very fine silvery threads. It clung to her body as if part of her skin. It was so pretty; the way the threads caught the light as she moved. Her shoes were made from what looked like the shape of autumn leaves sewn around her feet. She was so tiny and dainty.

As Ruby began to follow Maha she took a last look at where she had woken. Turning back, she saw the crystal rock which she had laid her hand upon, but no sand and no ocean. Looking ahead to Maha, she gasped, "Oh my goodness!" The sight took her breath away. She gazed at the most beautiful sight, as far as her eyes could see. There she saw towering clusters of giant prisms of clear quartz crystals. They were towering above, surrounding them like a cave, and continued in front of her as the path wove its way through them. She looked up and could not see the night sky anymore, but what she saw amazed her. Crystals, stalactites, like natures chandeliers with their light bouncing from them to light up the crystal sky. "Maha where are we?" Ruby asked. "We are deep in the Crystal Caverns, Heart of the Earth, and I am here to guide you and protect you", Maha responded gently. "Come, we really must be on our way", she said, as she held out her tiny delicate fingers to take Ruby's hand.

As they began to walk, the first thing Ruby noticed was the ground. She leant down to feel its texture with her hand. It was so soft, like sand, but crystalline like powdered sugar. As it fell through her fingers she realized it was millions upon millions of tiny quartz crystals that had been ground up to form a crystal sand. Some pieces were larger than others. Ruby bent down to pick up a small crystal that had caught her eye. She held on to it and felt its purity and light in her hand. She felt energy surge through her being; filling her with hope. It seemed to amplify her thoughts. She felt clear, calm and suddenly very excited at what lay ahead of her. Maha turned to her and gave her a small amulet woven pouch. "This is for your crystal, the crystal of Spirit" she said. Ruby placed the crystal in the pouch and placed it around her neck.

Their path was reflecting from the light above; each particle reflecting its light upon another to form a glorious symphony of pure delight. In awe of the majesty that lay before her, Ruby set off on her quest.
As she watched Maha walking in front of her, leading the way through the caverns, she watched her walk as if gliding lightly upon the

earth; her feet barely connecting with the cavern floor. "Are you from the Crystal Caverns Maha? Ruby asked. Maha began to speak. "I was born from the Light. I was born to be your guide. It is my life's purpose. I am an Earth Fairy, a nymph and a traveler between realms. I am guide of the elemental realms and I possess the ancient knowledge to pass through. I have been waiting for you Ruby".

Ruby was silent. "Waiting for me? But why?" she wondered. She took in everything Maha had said. Ruby had always had a love for the elementals, and felt a connection from when she was a young girl. She would always speak with the fairies and the trees, call to the sky and the moon, and here she was following beautiful gentle Maha; trusting her to lead her; but to where, she was unsure.

Maha and Ruby continued to walk, and as they did, Maha spoke of many things. Ruby listened to her story. "I have dedicated my life to this knowledge. It is my pledge from when I am born till the day I pass. I shall be returned", Maha continued. Ruby was taken aback, honored to have such a magnificent beauty to be her guide, but wondered, 'Guide to where?"

Maha continued to talk as they walked through the towering prisms of sparkling crystals, absorbing the magnificent pure energy the cavern held. "Earthlings are losing their ability to connect with the Spirits of the Earth. To connect, one must gain a spiritual connection and true authentic contact with the nature spirits. Eyes must be open to the sacred wisdom, and hearts must be open to pure love and one's spirit remain true. Respect of the elemental spirits will allow divine manifestation of our hearts desire. Purity of heart."

Maha continued, "Every place has its own spirit; its own power. You have arrived here to discover yours. It is your time, Ruby, it is time for you to be able to discover your true authentic self so you can spread your love with pure heart and journey on to discover your souls purpose, as I will mine.

CHAPTER SIX

As they began to near the last of the caverns' towering prisms, Ruby looked ahead and could see a clearing, and a forest of very old trees surrounding the area. Maha led the way to the centre of the clearing and looked around. Ruby followed, feeling the air brush upon her skin as she walked outside of the cavern. She looked up at the ancient trees, looking up into the night sky. It was littered with stars, shining like diamonds, glistening their light down for Ruby and Maha to see. It looked so much like the night sky on the golden sands; the stars so large and bright against the dark night sky.

The ground below her feet was now earth; no more sparkling crystalline powder, it was now the earth Ruby had always known. The clearing had four large stone pointed pillars as if they were the markings on a compass for North, South, East and West. In the centre was a flat stone pillar. This centre stone was lower, acting as an altar in the middle of the clearing.

Ruby followed Maha into the centre. Maha stood on one side of the centre altar and slowly began moving her feet, as if planting herself into the ground. She began to sway slowly, lifting her feet side to side in a gentle stomping motion, and as she did, she looked across to Ruby. Ruby stood opposite Maha with the altar between them, and did the same with her feet; grounding herself into the cool damp earth. She allowed her body to feel at ease and she began to sway side to side, slowly moving her hips to the motion. As they looked across at each other, Maha closed her eyes and raised her hands up to the sky. Ruby felt a little self-conscious at first as she raised her arms to mimic Maha and reached for the stars; each star twinkling at her as she began to close her eyes.

They began to sway and gently move their feet in unison. Ruby felt her long blonde hair gently swaying on her back as she lifted her feet in rhythm with Maha. It was then that Maha opened her mouth slightly and began to release a sound that Ruby could only imagine angels could make. It was a high angelic, continual pitch. It filled the air, the clearing and the forest into the night sky. Ruby was still swaying, and she began to feel their pace gaining harmony and a faster deeper rhythm. Side to side, their feet stomped heavier now as Maha continued her high vibrational pitch.

Ruby began to feel an immense energy passing through her body, connecting her into the earth; the energy rising through her body and out through her finger tips until it felt like it was reaching to the sky and looping back down through Maha and continuing around again. Time after time, this cycle continued as they swayed, stomping their feet side to side through the vibrational tone.

Ruby could feel Maha's energy connection and the purity of her angelic notes through her body. She could feel the ancient trees, their energy, greatness, power and knowledge from times gone by. She felt the power the earth beneath was now holding; the rhythm and the air around her pulsating like a drumbeat, breathing in the energy surrounding her. She allowed it to flow throughout her body. They had created an energy so powerful, flames began to surround them in a circle. The altar in between them became intensely hot and a flame grew from the centre. Meanwhile, Maha was still swaying, stomping, and calling to the skies; releasing the vibrational tone that pierced the night sky.

Ruby was still reaching for the sky; eyes closed. She continued to sway in a state of trance with no control of the surrounding elements, and began to feel warmth around her and in front of her. Heat - real heat – was so close to her as she swayed to the fast rhythm of Maha's beat. Ruby began to lose control and feel a crippling fear. She felt as if everything was closing in on her, and was in a state of panic as she frantically swayed and stomped, mimicking Maha's rhythm as if she was trapped and could not break free.

Ruby could feel her body beginning to vibrate in an unpleasant way now, as if releasing some unknown past that didn't belong; past fears and obstacles, and past lives that had blocked her from moving on.

She began to relive years upon years of fear and trauma. She felt regrets and sadness, and felt like she was trapped and had nowhere to go. Reaching, swaying and stomping, she reached for the sky as if reaching for some brightness, some help, but she had no control of this beast that was trying to break free. It was then she began to let out a primal scream from deep within her soul. She was releasing the heat, the fear, and the unknown; the flames grew around them so high, and the heat so intense as she released. Ruby screamed in a guttural sound that she could not control and had no idea where it was coming from. Her mouth opened as she let go, letting it all flow into the night sky. She began to cry uncontrollably and the swaying had begun to slow down; her feet stable upon the earth once more.

Ruby was slowly rocking and crying. She cried until she could cry no more, and felt a deep, deep sense of exhaustion. She became aware of the beat pounding in her head and her body still swaying slowly now; her eyes closed and swollen from what felt like an eternity of tears that had washed down her face. She collapsed into herself upon the ground.

Ruby had not known how long she was laying there, all curled up with hair strewn upon the earth. She uncovered her eyes slowly to see Maha once again kneeling above her. But her eyes went from Maha to another being who was standing above with fiery long red hair, course and thick as if she had stepped straight out from the Irish countryside. Ruby got shakily to her knees and knelt next to Maha, realizing this must be someone of great importance as she watched Maha bow her head to the red-haired woman. Ruby also bowed her head in respect. As they knelt in the circle, the flames around them had begun to subside to a deep orange glow, but the heat could still be felt. The four stone pillars began to take on a glow inside the circle of flames.

"Stand, beautiful ones", the woman said to Maha and Ruby. As they stood, she began to speak, "I am Drisana, Daughter of the Sun, Goddess and Keeper of Fire". "Come, beautiful one", she beckoned to Ruby. Drisana was stunning and wildly beautiful. She was tall and slim, and her body was clothed in a long fitted gown in colors of fire; glowing reds and oranges. The bottom of her dress was covered in tiny jewels resembling the colors of glowing embers; her long sleeves coming to a point on her hand where she wore rings of the most magnificent colors of Citrine and Amber. She gently allowed Ruby to stand and beckoned to her. She held her in a warm gentle embrace. Ruby felt such compassion and release. Her exhaustion was clear to all.

Drisana walked around the circle of flames, now lower and darker amber in color. She stopped opposite the group of ancient trees in the forest and began to speak louder to all around her. The clearing was silent as Drisana spoke out: "Let it be known to all who have entered here, they have entered into the circle of love and truth". With that, she held up her right hand and made a cutting motion in the air, creating a cross; a doorway to enter and to exit the circle. Drisana turned back to the circle and walked clockwise around the inside. She held her arm out above the flames. The flames grew and she touched them, reigniting them with the palm of her hand as she continued around the circle. The flames grew in height and heat, lighting up the clearing in an orange glow.

She stopped and turned to the first rock pillar." I call upon Guardians of the North, Earth. I call upon you to watch over us so we may be at peace, with love and healing". As she moved around the circle alighting the flame with her hand, she moved to the next stone pillar turning to it. "I call upon Guardians of the East, Air. I call upon you to bless us with your strength and inspiration, hear our heartfelt wishes and weave them upon the wind." She continued to the next pillar, the flames growing higher as she walked. Drisana stopped at the third pillar. "I call upon Guardians of the South, Fire. I call upon you to transform negative energies, allow positive growth and the strength to face our obstacles and fears". With that she continued walking around to the last pillar. "I call upon the Guardians of the West, Water. I call upon you to cleanse us, wash away resentments and feelings that no longer serve us." She turned and came back to the centre of the circle to the altar and its glowing flame licking at the night air.

CHAPTER SEVEN

Drisana stood back and asked Ruby to follow her. She took Ruby's hand in hers and led her to the point of exit, and they walked to the largest ancient tree towering above them on the forest edge. Maha remained in the circle as Drisana led Ruby over to the towering trees. Darkness through the forest made the flame circle light up the clearing behind her.

"These are ancient Ash trees", Drisana told Ruby. "They watch and serve us daily. They are our nature spirit guardians throughout all realms and all lifetimes, they hold the ancient knowledge. Their roots hold the knowledge of the world, the underworld and their trunks and branches the messengers to the heavens. They provide us with shelter, wood, oxygen and shade, for these we cannot live without. They are a symbol of all things safe and secure, and they are our key to reconnect with the sacredness of life and all living things. This, we must respect and treasure. The mighty Ash trees are our link to healing and transformation. They form our destiny, and they know our truth." "I would like you to ask them to release their gift to you Ruby", she said. "You will know what to ask. Be at one with the trees." Ruby looked back at Maha in the circle who gently nodded and then she looked back to the wide ancient tree.

As she neared the sacred tree she felt its magnificence, its magnitude and its many, many years of watching the worlds go by, as it slowly grew in wisdom and strength. She faced the tree and put both her palms upon the tree. It was cool. She felt the texture of the bark under her hands. As she touched the tree she looked up, straight up under the canopy of branches and could see the night sky and a scattering of stars through the leaves. Ruby leant closer and put her arms around the wide trunk. She could only manage to reach a third of the way around the massive tree trunk but found herself relaxing into embracing this magnificent being. She was silent, she was calm, and she closed her eyes as she rested the side of her head against the trunk. As she relaxed she felt a few leaves fall around her, as if a sign that the tree was ready to share with her its powers and give a part of itself to her. "It was a sign", she thought. Ruby let herself be one with the tree, allowing it to absorb her thoughts, her feelings, and her innermost soul voice.

She felt this magnificent gift of spiritual power fill her with uplifting joy and the gift of connectedness to the living essence of this beautiful tree. The tree spoke to her through her thoughts: "I am the foundation of the universe. My roots run deep and strong. They span from the lower world, nourishing me so I can offer empowerment. My trunk holds energy and those to come whom are worthy shall be given a sacred gift if they are pure of heart. My branches and leaves are my sight, my connection to the upper world, my gift to the earth as they fall and nourish my roots. This cycle will go on forever. This is why I hold the gift of destiny". "Accept my gift to you on your journey and use it wisely. I am blessing you with healing and reconnecting you with the sacredness of life. Live your truth, Ruby."

As Ruby held her arms around this spiritual power, its roots connecting far below, she felt every word, every blessing, and felt she had connected with something so very sacred, so ancient, and so wise. She thanked the tree, promising to honor her truth, and live life with zest and enlightenment. She would seek out all and honour the gift with devotion.

As Ruby gently released her hold around the trunk and stepped back, her right hand still connecting to the tree, she felt a wave of sadness leaving and had an instant urge to hug the tree once again. She did this time with a hug fit for a loved one she hadn't seen for a long, long time. "Thank you, thank you", she whispered to the tree. She stood back once again, looking up at its mighty branches; its eyes to the world. "Could it see me?" she wondered.

At that moment, as if in slow motion, a branch dropped next to Ruby. She went to pick it up, thinking to herself that is was just a branch, just a sign from the tree. But as she picked it up, it was like no other branch she had seen. It was so smooth, yet etched with a secret script. A language that was unknown to her was etched onto it. She was carrying a miniature staff. "How wonderful", she thought, as she walked to the centre of the circle to see Drisana and Maha waiting for her. She held out her Ash wand to show them. She was very pleased with her beautiful gift from the mighty ancient Ash tree. She had two gifts now: the quartz crystal in her bag and her wand. She felt very honoured.

Drisana told Ruby how wonderful a gift her wand was, but that she must now initiate it through fire. "Ruby, you must pass the wand through the flame, then around you ten times. Sprinkle it with this sacred water from the springs I hold, pass it through the air ten times, and touch the earth ten times."

As Ruby walked to the edge of the inside circle she began to pass her Ash wand through the flames; back and forth, counting to ten. Drisana walked to her and as she sprinkled water from a small vessel onto the wand, she chanted, "Through Fire, Water, Air and Earth, I consecrate this wand in the name of the Spirit and the Elementals". Ruby waved her wand, passing it through the air ten times and then down, touching the earth ten more times. She held it tight and brought it to her chest. When she had finished this ritual, Drisana beckoned to hold the wand and Ruby passed it to her. They watched as Drisana, Goddess of Fire, walked around the inside of the circle holding the wand above the flames, but not touching them. As she did this, Ruby watched the small flames begin to shrink and harden, turning into flame rock. They still glowed as they hardened; the colour of embers. Drisana continued around until she had returned to the centre altar. She held the wand above the flame and thanked the Guardians of the Elementals for allowing courage and strength to prevail, and to continue with the blessings of fire.

The flame in the centre began to solidify into a magnificent cluster of Amber prisms. Ruby gasped at the transformation. Drisana passed the wand back to Ruby. "You must choose one, Ruby. Your element of Fire." Ruby leant down, touched the cluster and chose a brilliant stone. She held it in her hand, feeling its warmth subsiding. Marveling at its beauty, she put it into the amulet bag around her neck, along with her quartz, and turned to Drisana and Maha. Drisana spoke: "This wand will be your channel to healing power and will allow you to overcome obstacles. It will offer you protection. It will be your guide home. You are now gifted with a powerful healing tool. You have been gifted with FIRE. Live your truth beautiful one, and go forth. Courage be with you, Ruby". Drisana leant forward and gently kissed Ruby between the eyes.

Drisana walked to the space she had crossed with her arms in the air as they walked out of the circle, closing the circle to complete the gift. It was now a dark orange, amber stone circle, glowing in the dark clearing. Ruby turned back to speak, but Drisana was nowhere to be seen. There was only Maha, who stood at the base of the Ash tree. Ruby joined her, and together they headed into the dark forest

CHAPTER EIGHT

The forest floor was littered with soft fallen leaves beneath their feet. Ruby had become weary and asked to rest. Maha seemed to be eternally blessed with boundless energy, but Ruby had become extremely tired. She could not remember the last time she had eaten. As they walked amongst the forest, the canopy of the trees allowed shards of light from the stars through, lighting their path. They found a group of large stones to stop at and sat as they leant their backs upon the stones. "Ah, bliss!" thought Ruby. She put her wand down next to her and took the small pouch from around her neck. She looked into her bag, hoping for some miraculous meal to appear. She had nothing but the crystals. Maha took her bag from around her neck and opened it. She took out a small bundle wrapped in a calico-like material, tied with vine. As she untied the vine, she placed the material on the ground and offered Ruby what looked like dried berries. "Thankyou", Ruby said gently, and took a few in her hand. She popped one into her mouth and was surprised at how it expanded and released the most amazing flavour as she began to chew. "Oh my goodness, these are delicious! What are they?" Ruby asked. Maha replied with a smile on her face, "They are Bloom berries". "Bloom berries? I've never heard of those before", Ruby stated as she reached for another one. They were a plum colour and oh-so-delicious. Very juicy, too. Maha told Ruby of how they gather Bloom berries in spring, and harvest and dry them. "They are a staple food supply to our people. They sustain us and give us nourishment. Please eat up." Ruby was fascinated listening to Maha's stories of the harvest and the folk who collect them. She wondered if she would meet Maha's people. After several Bloom berries, Ruby was so satisfied. She felt very full and as Maha had mentioned, nourished. She leant against the rock and began to close her heavy eyelids.

Ruby woke as the first ray of light touched her face. She was laying on her side, curled up against the stones. She opened her eyes and saw her bag and wand close by. She sat up and yawned, and had a good stretch. Maha was nowhere to be seen. She stood and turned around, and looked back to where they had come from. It looked very different in the dawn of light; the sun's rays just rising, shooting light through the forest floor and illuminating the trunks of the trees. The tips of the leaves shone as if to say "Good morning, world!"

Ruby stroked her dress down, gathered her wand and popped her pouch around her neck. She looked towards the sunrise and could make out someone coming towards her from a distance. She knew at once it was beautiful, delicate Maha gliding over the forest floor; so petite and dainty. As she got closer, she smiled at Ruby. "Good morning, Ruby? Did you sleep well? she asked. "Yes I did. I feel so refreshed, Ruby replied. "Well, we must be on our way then", said Maha. As they walked, the forest floor was so soft underfoot. Ruby was welcoming the sun's beams of light and warmth into her body. Every step she took was as if a spotlight was lighting her up. She cherished the sun shining its beams through the openings in the trees. The forest began to thin out after they had been walking for some time, and as they came to the edge of it, they could see as far as the horizon. They saw a meadow of long wavering grass as high as Ruby's knees, dotted with colourful blooms.

With the sun above and the sky so blue, it was a glorious sight ahead. Maha seemed to have a sprightly bounce in her step as she made her way through the meadow. Here and there, blooms were ready to burst open. Ruby saw bluebells nodding in the gentle breeze, as if they were welcoming her. Their joyous nature was inviting her to stop and watch as they seemed to play to and fro in the grass. She noticed tiny, pale blue forget-me-nots spreading their way through the grass, saying, "Follow me, I am pretty and small yet you shall not forget me". They reminded Ruby of her dear grandmother who always finished off her letters to Ruby with, "Forget me not". She was a kind, lovely woman and Ruby missed her greatly.

They made their way across the meadow, and it was so vast in every direction she looked. Maha kept turning back smiling, as if she was enjoying the nature delight before their eyes. Ruby saw many other flowers she had recognised before. She spotted tiny white daisies, bright yellow daffodils and brilliant red poppies, all waving in the breeze, happy to be soaking up the glorious warmth of the sun. Ruby was stopped in her tracks when Maha turned quickly and held up one hand as if to say, "Hush, stop!" As they quietly neared, they saw a gathering of rocks. Ruby had to hold her hand over her mouth as she gasped; not knowing whether she was in shock or if she was delighted at what she was seeing.

She stared at the short, dumpy being with large flat feet and lumpy looking largish hands. He had a flat, wide face with a long chin covered by a beard, and was dressed in brown suit with a tiny belt which held very small tools. "Oh my, a Gnome!" gasped Ruby. "Yes", confirmed Maha, with a grin. "And what, may I ask, are you lovely ladies doing passing by here?" the Gnome asked as he looked up. "Hello, kind sir", Maha replied. "We are seeking the way to the Eternal Springs and must pass through".

With that, he held his stomach, threw his head back and laughed heartily. "The Eternal Springs?" he chuckled, "Do you know which direction to go, young lady?" Ruby had already fallen in love with this funny little Gnome. He was jovial and cute, and she was sure he was trying his utmost to be helpful.

"Yes", replied Maha, "but we do need to be on our way. We must reach it before nightfall". "Well", he said, "I'm sure you know what you're doing. Do you need me as a guide?" he asked, puffing out his chest. "My friends have left to harvest the bloom berries and gather the flowers we use for healing. I am left in charge of the village", he explained.

Ruby looked down. She could not see a village, but instead saw a group of rocks clustered together amongst the meadows grasses. "May I see your village?" Ruby asked. The Gnome looked at Ruby. "Of course you can! That's if you can see it!" he laughed. Ruby knelt and was keeping an eye on the Gnome as she looked at the rocks. "Just rocks…" she said to herself. She looked hard but she could see no village. She glanced at the Gnome and he looked back at her enquiringly with a big smirk on his face.

"Close your eyes, child and wish it", he whispered. Ruby closed her eyes and as she did, she reached out her hand to steady herself on the rock. She felt like something had struck her mind's eye. "Use that place between your eyes where you can allow your physical vision to see the truth", he guided. She could see! She could see! Ruby began to speak out loud: "I can see a village! I can see doorways into the rocks, and windows. Oh, my!" she gasped, "It's so wonderful, like a village from a fairytale!" Ruby was so excited she took her hand away and lost sight. She opened her eyes and looked at the Gnome, and then back to the rock. "That was truly amazing. Thank you for allowing me to see your home", she said gratefully.

The Gnome spoke: "I think the lesson here today young lady, is do not believe everything you see. You must feel. Feel with your heart and mind. There are so many things we choose not to see. We close our mind's eye, but they lay right before us, waiting for us to discover them". Ruby bent down, and with her thumb and forefinger, reached out for his lumpy hand and shook it very gently. "Thank you so much. I am honoured to see." She stood up and said goodbye, carefully bypassing the rock area and made her way back into the wavering grass. As she looked back, she could not see the rocks anymore. They had blended into the grass.

CHAPTER NINE

As Ruby and Maha began to reach the edge of the meadow, they could see more trees ahead. These were birches, with their white trunks and fine dark branches swaying gently as they caught the warm breeze. Their leaves were a mixture of dark greens and silver. They began their walk through the Birches, with Ruby admiring them. Maha lead the way, and as they got deeper into the trees it had become darker. The sun was barely able to get through now, caused by the canopy of both birches and willow trees. The soft weeping willows' branches draped down like soft brooms sweeping the earth. Ruby could hear water flowing as they made their way through the overhanging branches. The willow trees were a sign that there was water close by, usually growing along the banks of streams and rivers.

They came to an opening in the trees and stopped on an embankment of fine river sand. Ruby and Maha saw before them a very wide river with rocks jutting out here and there; washed smooth from the rivers continual current. Ruby could see across to the embankment on the other side. It seemed a very long way away. The river was wide and although not flowing fast and rapid, it still had a considerable current.

The sun seemed to be leaving them now, disappearing through the trees and making its way to its night rest. Dusk was approaching; the skies producing shades of dark orange and reds, and the last few glints of magenta light shone through onto the water.

Maha turned to Ruby. "We must cross to the other side. There is no other way around." Ruby looked to Maha and studied her. She looked too delicate to swim; her skin and silken clothes too fine to get wet, and Ruby began to worry. Maha spoke: "Ruby, I can make it to the other side. I can fly." Ruby gave Maha a look of disbelief. She had followed her for miles upon miles and there was no sign of wings. As if Maha was reading Ruby's mind, she held her arms up to her sides, her palms facing upwards. She straightened her body up, held her head high, and what Ruby had thought all along was a silken cape begun to extend out to be the most magnificent wings she had ever seen. They were not unlike a dragonfly's wings - fine, long and delicate with iridescent silvers and blues shimmering throughout as they unfolded before her. The sun's final rays caught upon them and reflected their brilliance.

Ruby took a step back as they seemed to take up so much room. They were resplendent. They began to flutter gently and rise up and down, slowly lifting Maha from the ground. "I cannot carry you Ruby, I am too small. You must make your way across to meet me. I will be waiting for you. Allow the waters to wash away what no longer serves you. Blessings, dear Ruby", she said as she rose gently into the air and hovered for a short time. She took flight like a bird - gracefully and slowly - looking back at Ruby on the shore.

Ruby stood there in awe. She watched Maha until she reached the other side of the river and gently landed upon the embankment. Maha was tiny but now looked even smaller and so far away. Ruby could not call to her as the sound from the water flowing was rushing in her ears. It was then that she froze in fear. The realisation that she had to cross deep water. It was her biggest fear.

She stood frozen to the spot. She could not move as she felt her heartbeat getting stronger until it filled her ears. Her heart beat was louder and stronger and she felt fear setting in; the type of fear where she wanted to flee. To where - she did not know. She could not turn back. She had to cross and she had nowhere to return to! Fear turned to panic, panic turned to anxiety and she began to tremble as she felt she was getting flushed and out of breath; everything becoming a blur. She began to count her breathing "In...1,2,3,4...Out 1,2,3,4...In 1, 2, 3, 4..." and did this until her heartbeat settled a little. She stood on the bank for what seemed like forever, trying to avoid the inevitable. She could swim, but as she had become older there seemed something about the depths of dark water that terrified her.

As she stepped forward, she dipped her toes into the water. It was now getting shadowy as the sun was going down. It made the water look gloomier, which frightened her even more. She looked across and saw a large rock jutting out from the water. "I may be able to swim to that for a rest", she thought. "Yes, that's what I will do. Face my fears", she told herself. As she immersed herself in the water she felt the temperature: not too cold, but cool. It took her breath away at first, but she got used to it as she was contemplating her next move. She held her wand and decided to tie it with the straps that held her amulet pouch. She felt in her pouch, made sure her crystals were still safely in there, and slung the pouch over her back.

Ruby was now free to swim. She walked in to the deeper water and could feel the current of the water pulling her downstream a little, but her feet were firmly planted onto the rocks at the bottom of the riverbed. With her heart beating fast, she took a final look towards the other shore to Maha who was watching her. She took a big deep breath and plunged in. She was unsure what was under the darkening water, so she held her hand forward as she kicked to get some distance. She could feel the pull of the current as her feet had left the bottom.

Ruby rose to the surface, took another breath and returned her head under to swim and kick as hard as she could. Using her strokes to gain distance, she found the current was fierce; much stronger than she had realised. It began to drag her sideways down the stream. She kicked and kicked to regain her position and began to feel as if the water was rolling her over as she travelled downstream, unable to maintain her balance. Panic set in again. Breathing hard and fast, she gasped for air and the water pulled her further away and deeper into the current.

Exhausted, Ruby kept getting glimpses of the shore line but could not see Maha. She had travelled too far downstream now, and knew she was in trouble. She tried to float but was beginning to tire. She felt heavy and started to sink. Ruby was too weak, and she had become disorientated. Her strength was deteriorating fast, and she began to let go. She opened her eyes under the water and saw nothing but darkness as she held on to her last breath; her cheeks blown out seeking that last gasp of air from within.

She had no choice but to let go. Ruby opened her mouth in desperation to breathe. She gasped and writhed, and in flooded what seemed like gallons of water that filled her nose, mouth and throat. She was fighting, twisting and screaming under the water. Ruby closed her eyes, preparing herself for the end, and let her body go limp to allow the last wave of water to flow through her lungs and as she did, she felt a hand grab hers. She opened her eyes, still hanging on to what felt like the last second of life she had left, and felt her body go lifeless.

Ruby felt the water drain from within her body as if a vacuum was attached to her mouth emptying her lungs. She felt this being filling her limp body full of oxygen; filling her lungs as if they were about to explode and her body began to gain strength. They were still under the water and the being began to pull away from Ruby's face but still held her hand. Ruby shook her head. "Please no, don't go", she called out. Ruby had spoken underwater! She opened her mouth slightly and realised she could breath. The being that saved her was long and sleek, had fin-like skin with gills at the side of her neck, and her body shone with a bluey-green iridescence. Her eyes were a piercing electric blue, and her hair golden just like Ruby's. She didn't have one fin like a mermaid, although her legs were covered in iridescent scales and resembled a fin.

As they looked at one another, Ruby noticed their blonde hair floating around their faces like satin in the water, and was still in awe of the fact that she was truly able to breath freely under the water. Ruby was not drowning; she was just like the merperson in front of her. "Thankyou", said Ruby as her words bubbled up through the deep water. "Thank you for saving me. I am forever in your debt". "Do not be in my debt, sweet girl", replied the merperson. "You have faced your gravest fear with such courage and strength".

The merperson continued, "My name is Asrai. I am a Naiad, a river nymph. I am here to cleanse away and wash away your fears, those that no longer serve you. In this you must accept and be healed of these fears. That is all I ask of you". "You have made a brave decision to cross these waters, for it is only the brave who face their fears. In doing so, you will restore your strength and spirit. You will have the power to face other fears."

As Asrai spoke, it was like a tune coming from her mouth. Ruby felt at ease and trusted her completely. She had heard stories of merpeople dragging people down in the water but now she knew why; they were here to save us. The Mermaids from the oceans, the Naiads from the rivers, the Undines, the water people, those that have saved so many souls.

Asrai took Ruby's hand and with a swift flick of her legs pulled Ruby along in the water, so fast, darting around in and out of the rocks. It was a wonderful feeling; the sensation of the water rushing around her body and being able to breathe, releasing bubbles of joy as they dove deeper and deeper. As they continued, Ruby could see the bottom of the river. They were so deep now, and it was very dark, although a sight to behold was the riverbed lit up with glowing minerals, like a wonderland under the water. The mineral deposits were glowing iridescent blues, greens and turquoise. Ruby swam amongst them, marveling at the illumination. They resembled hundreds upon hundreds of glowing treasures all along the river floor. Asrai gestured Ruby to choose one. Ruby swam and admired them all until she settled for one that was rounded and the size of her palm. She picked it up from the riverbed and held it in her hand. It pulsed, it glowed, and it was transparent blue and so pretty.

Asrai told Ruby she had chosen Aquamarine: "A wonderful crystal for compassion and strength of character; both of which you possess". Ruby held the crystal as they swam upwards, looking back on the wonderland below her. The lights faded as they ascended. Asrai came up to the surface pulling Ruby behind her. They stayed bobbing in the water, and the current didn't seem to move them now at all. Asrai's strength held them stationary as they approached the shallows. As she guided Ruby to the shore, they could see Maha flying low above the water towards them. She had spotted them and came down to land upon the shoreline in front of Ruby. Asrai swam with Ruby to where the water met the shore and in parting, said to Ruby, "Travel safe brave one, you have overcome many things. You have strength and courage to go on. You have washed away your fears to see a beautiful new light. Bless you, Ruby."

Asrai turned to go and dove deep, back into the water. Ruby was still sitting in the shallows on the shore. She turned to look up at Maha. Maha looked down at her with a look in her eyes that was full of respect and acknowledgment. It was the kind of look that a parent has for their child knowing they cannot interfere, but only watch as the child learns the lessons of life. The true look of love.

CHAPTER TEN

Ruby walked from the water as Asrai disappeared into the depths of the river. Maha looked at Ruby with a deep knowing between them and Ruby felt the powerful force of their souls and spirit connecting, their energies bonding without words. Ruby stood there still wet, but not cold; the warm night breeze drying her. She stood on the bank of the river for a moment. Dusk was now upon them. She put her hand up to her chest and felt her amulet pouch. Her crystals were still there and her wand was still safe within its net, as it slung over her shoulders. She opened the pouch and placed the water crystal safely with the others. They had protected her; of that she was certain. She held them both tightly, believing in their power and most importantly, believing in herself.

She kissed them both quickly, as if to bless them for her next adventure. Ruby didn't know where she was going, but knew it would certainly be another test of her will, no matter what she experienced. They were all making her stronger, more aware, and empowering her. Yes! She felt empowered, proud and free.

Maha had found a small hollow amongst some bushes and rocks not far from the riverbank, and Ruby joined her. Ruby dreamt that night of the Moon. She was able to fly. She was flying high, then dipping down like an eagle; soaring and gliding on the winds. With her mighty wings, she flew above the golden shore line, following it within her sight until she swiftly turned and rolled in the air like a stunt pilot. Her wings were carrying her wherever she desired. She curved to fly back amongst the stars, reaching out and touching them as she passed. She was making her way towards the brilliant glow of the moon.

Ruby woke with the sunshine streaming in through the trees and beaming on her face. She lay there for a moment soaking in its warmth and behind her eyelids, could see brightness flickering. She was not displeased when she opened her eyes to see the wonderful daybreak that was just beginning.

The sun, upon waking was painting the sky like an artist; splashes of yellow, oranges and soft pinks. As she rose, she found Maha offering her some bloom berries from her calico bag. Ruby gladly accepted and devoured their lushness. "Delicious", said Ruby.

"What a wonderful, bright morning", Ruby marveled. She ran her hands over her hair, still silken and soft, and so long as she pulled it over her shoulder stroking it. As she did, she noticed the spiral design on her hand and with her finger, traced over the design on her right hand. She sat in silence for a long time, and then spoke quietly, "Maha? May I ask you something? I just, I just," she began to stutter as her words came out. I just don't understand what has happened to me. I mean, I'm sure, but I can't remember. But, I feel…" she went on, "I feel I'm different? I don't know how to explain this looking at my hair and my body. It is mine, yet it's so different to what I think, what I remember. Am I remembering me as another? I don't understand at all. I am very unsure of who I am and where I belong". Maha looked up at Ruby with her magnificent amethyst eyes and it was some time before she began to answer. Ruby could tell that what was going to be said was being thought about very carefully.

Maha began, "We are all born to experience life. Its lessons, its losses and its loves. We are born to serve ourselves and that of a higher realm. Our intuition, spirit and soul is passed down from life to life no matter which life we are in. Whether we access this awareness depends on if you were born to relive and learn from these lessons to become of higher guide to others." Maha paused. "We of higher realms have power to travel dimensions. Only those pure of heart and soul, those that have been chosen, those who are to learn, believe and serve their higher self. Those who can share this love and light that comes from within. Some are not ready to complete their journey throughout the realms. They will take these lessons into other lives and maybe one day, they will find their calling and so it will begin. We can only guide those who hold life sacred to open themselves up to face their own transformation and destiny. You have crossed many, many realms throughout the ages."

Maha looked at the sky, and then to Ruby. "You have been chosen, Ruby. You have been chosen for reasons only you will discover on your life's path. I also have been chosen in this realm to be your guide. We are connected now, and in another realm, we will be connected again. We may look different, but we will know when we meet. We will feel the connection - a soul connection, bound by trust and of the heart. You feel different because this is your time to experience the lessons in this realm to allow you to raise your vibration to a higher level; to be able to live your truth."

Ruby sat for a long time taking in all Maha had said. It was a lot to digest, but yes, so much of it made sense to her, and yet she still was unsure. So much had happened. It was all so overwhelming and frightening, yet powerful at the same time. The reality was, Ruby was here sitting opposite the most beautiful soul, listening to this explanation. She would have to allow time to pass so that each day she was more understanding; more aware of this shift. Deep down she believed she was still learning about herself. She did understand. Yes, she truly understood.

They gathered up the cloth containing the bloom berries, tied them up and left the hollow to begin their walk from the woods. They followed alongside the river for miles, then took a turn leading them onto a path which left the water behind them. Ruby could hear the noise of the river subside as they made their way through the winding forest. The sun was streaming through the birch trees, the skies above so blue. What a glorious day. She felt very light and happy.

CHAPTER ELEVEN

As Ruby and Maha came to the edge of the trees they discovered a sudden drop; they had come to a ridge of the mountain. They could see a valley below. The view was spectacular. Ruby looked down into the valley below and saw shades of green, like a patchwork quilt. In the distance was a range of mountains; the largest with it peak hiding amongst the fluffy white clouds. Maha stopped and looked towards the mountain range. "It is there", she said, pointing to the mountain with its peak covered in clouds, "that we need to head for."

It seemed obvious to Ruby that they must descend into the green valley rather than walk all the way around this ridge which led away from the mountains. Far below, Ruby could see that the river they had been following had turned into a stream, weaving its way through the valley. She followed the stream with her eyes to see that it became a marshland. As she looked, she saw lights flickering out of the corner of her eye. She rubbed her eyes as the sun was now high in the sky, causing her to squint. Ruby glanced again and was sure she could see tiny lights glistening in the marshes. She focused her eyes. Yes, there they were; it was as if someone were holding a mirror and it was reflecting in the sun. The marshland was shimmering and twinkling with light. "Oh look, how beautiful", she said to Maha who was still studying the mountain range ahead. Maha walked over to see what Ruby had discovered. She also looked a few times before she abruptly spoke out. "You must not look. Do not look again, Ruby", she said quite sternly. Ruby was taken back. Maha had not spoken to her like that before. "Oh, but it's so pretty. Let's go that way. It looks so much nicer to walk through the valley", Ruby pleaded, "We can walk along the marshland to see the beautiful lights".

Ruby had already begun to steady her footing as she was making her first steps down the hill they had stood upon. She was mesmerized by the shimmering lights attracting her eye. She could not hear Maha calling her as she kept walking slowly, always looking up to see the glistening marshlands. She had not realized she was alone. She was unaware of anything but the marshes calling her. As she steadied herself, holding onto the steep craggy hill at her side, she was shocked to turn and Maha appeared in front of her in the air with her wings extended in all their glory. Her wing expanse was so wide. Maha was hovering just above Ruby and suddenly dropped down to be directly in front of her; so close in fact, that Ruby could feel the air from her wings making a draft upon her skin.

"Ruby", she spoke with a worried, but stern voice, "You must stop. You must turn back".

Ruby looked below Maha's wings to still see the marshlands beckoning her, and with that sight she took another step down. Maha was now so close, hovering with her wings moving quite frantically to keep Ruby from moving another step. "They are the Will-o-Wisps. They live in the marshes, and they are known to lure travelers with their charms. They lure them to harm. I cannot let you pass. Many a seeker has been taken, never to be seen again. They appear so beautiful and playful to attract you; like a moth to a glistening web. Ruby, I cannot let you go."

Maha continued, "I beg you to use your minds' strength and turn around. Listen to what I am asking, Ruby". Maha was now trying to block Ruby from taking another step forward with her wings but she was only tiny. She kept talking to Ruby to try and break the trance like state she had found herself in. Ruby desperately needed to see the lights, but she also felt her mind telling her to turn back. It felt like a desperate battle of good against evil. Ruby tried hard to break her vision of the Will-o-Wisps as they were calling to her with their beautiful lights. As Ruby turned slightly she broke vision with the marshes and her trance was interrupted. Maha had now lowered herself to the earth to be by her side. "Look at me, Ruby. Look into my eyes", Maha pleaded, gently.

Ruby looked at Maha, and as soon as she made contact with those amethyst pools of eyes, Ruby knew the truth. She turned back immediately and headed up the hill. "Oh Maha, please don't let me look back. I feel so weak", Ruby sighed. Maha promised Ruby and led her back to the crest of the hill where they had been standing not long before. They kept walking until the marshlands were out of view. Ruby had to sit down. Her head felt so heavy, she had a dull ache, and her eyes were sore.

"I am so sorry, Maha. I have let you down. I was lured. I'm not sure? Was it greed? I just wanted what I saw and thought nothing of you my friend", she said as she looked at Maha. Maha reassured Ruby that it was a natural thing and many before her had become so possessed by the lure that they had not been able to be saved. "You possess an inner strength and the most adamant quality of determination. They became your power. You did not let me down. You listened to your inner voice, and that's all I ask of you." Maha truly understood what strength it had taken to turn away. She put her tiny arm around Ruby's shoulder. "The Will-o-Wisps are very powerful. All temptation is powerful, Ruby. You are a strong woman. Let's not look back, but always look forward", said Maha with a smile on her face.

Ruby looked at her and gave her a weak smile. She was drained. She agreed as she stood to her feet.

As they slowly walked along the crest of the hilltop, they could see the skies becoming greyer with clouds rolling in. The winds had picked up slightly and the blue sky was now turning a shade of pale grey. Everything around them had taken on a different look. Trees and the bright green grasses below were now under the shadow of the darker clouds. The mountain peaks ahead were immersed in cloud. The skies above opened up and rain showers fell. They weren't heavy, but they were enough to send Ruby and Maha sheltering in a glade of trees. Maha and Ruby planned to wait out the showers and as they sat watching the clouds roll past and the rain fall, they began to plan their route to the mountain. They spoke for some time, realising it was going to take a long time to reach the largest mountain peak, as they had to walk around to the next valley and then climb.

With a small twig, they drew their map in the earth. They looked up to see a break in the clouds and the sun peaking its bright sunny face, sending cheer and warmth with it. They stood under the trees watching the rain showers become much lighter, until they stopped. Water slowly dripped from the leaves. As they moved out from the shelter of the trees to the grass that lay in front of them, the sight was nothing short of a miracle. From the edge of the hill in front of them arching over the valley below, there appeared the most magnificent rainbow, leading all the way to the mountain peak ahead. It was the most glorious sight Ruby had ever seen.

The colours were so deep, it looked like a bridge between worlds. Maha and Ruby approached the rainbow edge slowly. Like all rainbows, the colours blended into each other. It was a mirage of colour mists with reds, oranges, yellow, green, blues and violet.

Maha looked at Ruby, and she was already at the edge. She smiled. Ruby smiled back. Nothing had ever made her happier than rainbows, but never had she seen anything like this phenomenon that lay before her.

CHAPTER TWELVE

Ruby held her hand out towards the rainbow. She wasn't sure what would happen. She thought her hand would pass through this glorious coloured spectrum bridge. To her surprise however, she felt it, she felt the colours! She moved forward, intrigued by the feeling. Ruby placed both hands out in front of her. She was drawn in to the colour and its energy field.

She continued to walk through the mists, looking around, as it excited her senses. Ruby walked towards the red mist; she felt its power, its secret. The life force filled her body and mind, and she felt warmth and passion filling her senses. Her body was awake. As she left the red, the orange mists blended in, finding her experiencing visions upon visions of her creativity; so much vitality, she found her mind was exploding with ideas. With oranges blending into yellow, she walked through into visions of new beginnings. Ruby bathed in its glorious brightness and cheer, filling her with energy. She spun around like a little girl, dancing amongst the colours and moved from yellow to green. The mists here were a blend of glorious colours, like those of the peacock. Green was for growth and she felt a sense of deep peace. She was so content here. The veil of mist between greens and blue led her to experience the importance of communication and the feeling of deep healing. She felt it soaking into her very soul.

Nearing the violet, Ruby felt the power of ritual and profound spirituality. She began to reel from the myriad of colours and gifts; the energies combining and flowing through her. She wanted to run back through the colours and stay forever. "I must be in heaven", she thought. "This is surely where I am." She smiled and spun around, her arms now open wide, taking it all in, breathing in the colours around her. As she came to a standstill, she looked ahead and realised she was coming to the end of the rainbow. She had nearly reached the mountain, and as she neared the base, the colour mists began lessening in strength. Forward she walked, through a golden mist, and all the colours had come together for a final message. She stopped and inhaled the golden mist. Ruby's body was filled with a harmony, a spiritual high, that of the Divine. She had been blessed. She exhaled slowly and stepped from the mist to the mountain.

There was her companion; her wings out, landing gently on the mountain next to her. Ruby looked back as the clouds disappeared and the rainbow began to fade. The skies were now so blue and looking above them, the peak of the mountain was covered in those soft white fluffy clouds once again. Maha looked at the rainbow as it began to vanish, and said, "You have been given the highest blessing from Spirit". Ruby looked at Maha. She was feeling as light as a feather. She was speechless. She was on a spiritual high. "I was given a rainbow blessing", she replied to Maha. Maha nodded.

They looked above them to see the peak still covered in dense cloud. As they began their climb, the terrain was craggy and rough. It was steep, and as they neared the peak, they entered the cloud mass. Ruby could not see Maha around her. She kept climbing, holding on to the rocks and fallen logs. She stopped to regain her footing and catch her breath, and looked around again. She was amongst the clouds; so thick she couldn't see the ground in front of her. She climbed with caution, wary of loose rocks. She could hear the whistling of the wind, like tiny echoes in the mists. She thought she could hear voices. Ruby called out, but no one answered. "Maha", she called again, but all that came back was her echo.

She began to feel alone and concerned that she was heading in the wrong direction. "So long as I head upwards, I shall be ok", she thought to herself. Slowly and steadily, she climbed. She called out again, "Maha, Maha". A voice returned her call, soft and whispery coming from far away: "I am here, Ruby. I am here". "Where are you? I cannot see you", Ruby called out into the mist, her voice carrying on the wind. All she could see around her was that she was surrounded by a thick swirling mist.

"I am here Ruby", a voice said". "I am around you. I am the clouds, the air, and the wind. I am Auiroa, Guardian of the East, Wind, and Spirit Goddess of Air. Listen to the whispers on the wind, the messages you receive. Ask your questions, your answer will become clear. I am of the Sylphs, the Spirits of the Air, to bless you with vision and clarity. Listen to the messages and perceive what is relevant to your life. Be guided. Ask and you shall receive." Ruby could see no one, but she could feel the cool breezes upon her skin playing games gusting around her. She imagined the sylphs playing around her, chasing and diving creating breezes. She saw flashes from the corner of her eye, and yes, they were around her. She imagined she could see Auiroa's flowing cloak of air whisping about her as she climbed.

Ruby kept climbing as she spoke out loud: "Guardians of the East, send to me a guide, a guide from Air. Send to me the power of the Sylphs to aid and heal me. Bless me with the strength of assurance and the clarity of confidence. I feel you and welcome you. Please guide me now". The Sylphs began to play around her once again, whispering blessings to her upon the wind. They swirled and turned as they guided her to the summit. Just as she was nearing the top of the clouds, to her left through the thinning mist she saw beautiful Maha; her iridescent wings shimmering through the clouds. She called out, but there was no answer. Her wings were slowly coming into vision as they came closer. She could feel them creating a breeze as they neared her.

Ruby broke through the top of the cloud, held on and pulled herself up gripping onto the final rock, but it broke away in her hand. She pushed herself up with her foot and felt the sun begin to warm her face. There were blue skies above and the top of the peak was only a short distance away. Still gripping the rock piece in her hand, she studied it. It was aqua in colour. Her attention was taken away when she saw wings shimmering; iridescent and reflective of the light coming through the mists near her, and fly above her to the summit. It was not Maha at all. It was a giant dragonfly, in greens and blues with purple and silver throughout its magnificent wings. She looked up as it took flight, darting in different directions, then stopping midflight to hover. It was so large; it was creating a shadow. As she neared the summit, she sat watching this majestic creature show off above her. Such beauty and grace. Such a powerful being.

Ruby watched as it hovered one last time above her and then flew off into the horizon; diving back down into the mists. She looked back at the gemstone in her hand and realised it was a piece of Turquoise; a stone for clarity of the mind and a wonderful stone for bringing focus back to the heart centre. She placed it in her pouch. Ruby was tired and was waiting for Maha to appear. She had faith that she would; she had never let her down. Ruby lay down, her head upon her arm, and rested in the warm rays of the sun as it began to drop slowly in the sky. It wasn't long before she sat again, looking towards the sun. It was partly hidden under the clouds now. It had become late in the afternoon, the warmth slowly diminishing as it began to sink into the mists. She was looking directly at the tip of the sun on the horizon when she saw something glistening coming towards her. It seemed so far away, like a speck in the distance.

CHAPTER THIRTEEN

As it neared, Ruby called out: "Yes! Maha, Maha!" She stood waving her arms wildly. It was Maha, and flying with her was her friend the majestic giant dragonfly. It was a sight to behold; gleaming wings catching the last of the sun's rays and the colours of their wings. Maha looked so graceful and delicate. The giant dragonfly, so powerful and agile, both creating harmony in the skies. It was beautiful to watch their flight. As they neared, Maha gently lowered herself down to the ground. She settled upon the mountain top and with a soft shake of her body, her wings retracted behind her into her silver silken body. Maha looked up and called out in a soft angelic tone; barely a whisper to the winds. From high above came the dragonfly, darting and hovering in sight.

Maha spoke, "The Dragonflies are nature spirits, our most ancient Messengers of the Air. They bring love and joy; a new light to our being. When we see these beautiful souls, they hold messages from loved ones gone before us. Many, many life times before us. They have been flying between realms for three hundred million years, giving hope and love, allowing us to learn the deeper meaning of life. I am blessed to fly with such beings. We hold them with very high eminence. They are our Spirit Messengers. We are blessed to be in its presence.

As Maha finished speaking, she called out once again a soft message to the Spirit Messenger of Air. The dragonfly began to slowly and gently descend to the summit. Ruby was in awe in the dragonfly's presence. She studied its huge being; its head with such large eyes being able to sense movement and small antennae. Its long body was supported by two pairs of magnificent transparent iridescent wings; so powerful to be able to fly against strong winds, yet float on the lightest of breezes. The wings were made up of silvery veins; each one holding memories of ancient ones who had passed before; like a library of messages, kept by the Spirit Messenger of Air.

Ruby bowed her head to the dragonfly. She felt it looking at her, scanning her, drawing her memories and storing them in his wings; another chapter for the library of life. "Come, Ruby. We must hope the Guardians of the Air allow us to pass easily as we need to make haste. The dragonfly needs the warmth of the sun to fly", said Maha. Ruby watched as Maha shook herself gently, expanded her wings and fluttered up horizontally into the air above her. Ruby looked questionably at her. "I have no wings", she said. Maha turned to the dragonfly and back to Ruby. "Here are your wings of flight, Ruby" she said as she looked towards the Spirit Messenger of Air.

Ruby neared the dragonfly and walked under his outstretched wings gently vibrating above her. She looked at his elongated body, slowly put her hands up behind his wings and launched herself up onto his body. As she steadied herself, she looked down to the ground, her legs dangling either side of his long body. Maha told Ruby to hold on to where his wings extended from his trunk. There were small nodules where she was able to grip with her hands. Ruby hoped she was not harming him in any way. Maha rose higher above them now and began to level off. Ruby became aware of the sensation of high vibration and air coming from the wings either side of her. They were vibrating gently but gaining strength and power. They lifted off. Up and up they rose, remaining horizontal for a short time. Ruby looked down at the mountain summit, and glanced around her. All around her were open skies; the top of the sun disappearing behind the clouds below. They had risen above the mountain peak and turned to fly in a straight line beyond the peak. They were heading in the direction of the other mountains they had seen from the crest.

Ruby looked across at Maha flying beside them with her delicate wings. She was riding upon the breeze that was being created by the Spirit Messenger of Air. Ruby thought of the Air Sylphs and wondered if they were helping them now, feeling the air upon her face and brushing across her body as they flew above the clouds. She knew they were; she could hear them giggling and whispering in her ear as the giant wings beside her hummed. She held on tight as she felt they were descending towards the cloud. Ruby closed her eyes as they connected with the mist. Down they went, through thick cloud; much thicker than her ascent to the summit. She could not see in front of her as the mist was dampening her eyes. Ruby closed her eyes and held on as they dove deeper and deeper into the unknown. She let go of any fear and felt so much trust in this beautiful creature. She kept her eyes closed until she felt the damp mists break.

They were now flying under the clouds, the skies still a pale blue and the sun behind them still yet to set. Ruby felt that last warmth of the sun against her back drying her cotton dress and warming her dampened skin. She gazed forward to the Spirit Messenger's head; his eyes glistening like thousands of fragments joining - like a mirror or a jigsaw puzzle - so many eyes, so much wisdom, and so much vision; both past and future. Ruby settled and relaxed her tense shoulders as she flew high above the scenery below. Green fields led into expanses of wildflower meadows and rocky outcrops. "Maybe they were gnome villages", she thought to herself. She looked across at Maha who had fallen behind now. Her wings were delicate and not so powerful, but she was gliding along in the slip stream of the mighty Spirit Messenger of Air.

CHAPTER FOURTEEN

As darkness approached, the breeze cooling upon her skin, Ruby thanked the Sylphs for allowing them easy and safe passage. They had guided and accompanied the travelers for what seemed like hours now. Ruby had not felt their sudden playful twists and turns about her or the whispers in her ear for some time as they glided in the air. They were flying lower in the darkness, the stars above lighting their way as if a guided map in the heavens. The sight of the wings of the Spirit Messenger catching the moonlight in flight was so spectacular. There was darkness below them as Ruby looked down. She could not tell whether they were flying over grasslands or hills; she couldn't quite make out the landscape. She was unsure where they were. Maha was now by their side as they flew in unison; a sight to behold, her wings outstretched glimmering like thousands of fine silver threads catching the light, her tiny delicate body so light and graceful.

Maha pointed down to their right. Ruby looked down and felt them descending slowly. Ruby saw a cluster of tiny lights in the darkness far below. As they descended, the lights became brighter. It looked like a fairyland from above. They gently landed on the outskirts of the lights they had seen from above. Ruby dismounted from her magnificent Spirit Messenger of Air and went to stand in front of him. She bowed slowly to him. She began to thank him for his service to her: "Spirit Messenger of Air, I thank you for allowing me to fly high and feel the wind upon my skin, for allowing me to receive the gift of clarity and the whispering messages. I heard the answers to my questions spoken to me by the air spirits above. You are wise and gentle and I will never forget you. I will always know when I see your kind in this realm or another that you bring messages. You honour me with the gift of knowledge, peace and healing and messages from beyond. I shall always take comfort in this."

The Spirit Messenger of Air slowly bowed his giant head to Ruby and began the gentle hum of his mighty wings again. With his beautiful iridescent wings, Ruby watched as he ascended into the night sky. Ruby turned to see that Maha had been watching them in the darkness. Behind her lay a grotto of trees and a pathway some way off, lit by lanterns. As they neared the pathway, Ruby marveled at the lanterns. They were actually giant Lily of the Valley blooms on either side of the pathway; their stalks bending inwards to create an archway of lanterns above their heads. The soft light was created by fireflies busy underneath the blooms. "Oh, how sweet", Ruby exclaimed. She was thrilled to see such a pretty sight.

The arch of lilies lit the pathway before them until they rounded the corner of the trees. There in front of her, she saw a large village with earth nymphs just like Maha going about their nightly business. Some were crossing the narrow streets; some were going into homes. Ruby stopped to take in the sight. There were small, hut style homes built from earth and stone with each roof made from woven thatched branches and vine. Each hut looked warm and inviting, with a lantern dotted here and there throughout the streets. Some huts had smoke rising from their stone chimneys; the gentle puffs rising into the night sky.

As Ruby stepped into the village with Maha, the nightly bustle seemed to stop as if time stood still for that moment. The villagers looked towards them as Maha walked slightly in front of Ruby and made her way to what resembled a village centre, with its small raised platform, a lantern on each corner. Ruby felt all eyes upon her with their smiling faces gazing up at her in wonder. She was much larger than the Earth nymphs, which made her feeling slightly awkward. As she looked around at the crowd milling around the platform, she observed that these were the most beautiful looking beings she had ever seen. They were Maha's people. Maha had come home.

She saw earth nymphs, delicate and petite; both male and female. The females all had long, straight, silken hair of varying shades. The males also had long silken hair, pushed behind their slightly pointed ears. She had not noticed Maha's ears before as she had never seen her hair up to uncover them. The clothing worn by her people was made from the same silken threads Maha wore in varying soft shades. The females all wore robes shaped to their petite bodies. The males wore pants and tunic robes, and all wore shoes made from leaves sewn with vine thread into a point just like Maha's. Ruby looked at them all scanning her. Were they scanning her thoughts? She knew the power of Maha's amethyst eyes. Now she found she had a village of amethyst eyes peering at her; all of them varying shades of purple. Some were deep amethyst and some paler, all glistening in the lantern light.

Maha had moved a few steps forward in the centre of the platform and faced her people. She spoke. "My people, my Earth Sprites, people of my tribe and home. I have returned." With that, the crowd all raised their hands and cheered and clapped. Great excitement and a feeling of happiness spread through the crowd. Ruby found herself smiling at their joy. Smiles and chatter broke out amongst them. Ruby felt such joy for Maha and noticed the glow from her people. The collective energy was so uplifting. "Her tribe", she had called them. Maha loved her tribe and they loved her. Maha raised her hand once again and the chatter dispelled all eyes upon her.

"This is my dear beautiful one, Ruby", she said as she turned to Ruby. "We have journeyed together. I, as her chosen guide, as all earth nymphs are born to. It has been my honour and privilege to bring Ruby to our home." Maha smiled at Ruby. The crowd let out cheers of welcome. Ruby felt so happy to have been acknowledged by her tribe. She turned to the crowd of tiny beings and smiled. "Thank you. I am humbled", Ruby said. As the crowd began to disperse, Maha led Ruby to a little path behind the village, to a bigger building Ruby assumed was the town meeting place or hall. Maha knocked on the door and it was opened by two beautiful earth Nymphs. Maha lead Ruby through the door. The building was larger and roofline higher than the village homes, but Ruby still had to bow her head to walk through the double doors. Once she was inside, she was able to straighten up with the roof being very high pitched.

She looked around and saw lanterns gently flickering, candles lit and soft flowing curtains at the back corner of the hall. Maha was in the door but a minute when she was greeted so lovingly by the two nymphs. They crowded around her, hugging her and laughing. One was so excited to see Maha, that she jumped up and down with glee. From the rear of the hall from behind the curtains came a stunningly exquisite nymph. "Oh, Maha. How we have missed you, dear one", she said as she approached Maha and hugged her tightly. She was stunning. She had beautiful, long golden hair braided down her back with pretty white flowers placed in the braids, and the darkest amethyst eyes. She wore a pale mauve robe.

"Eaven, my beautiful fair one", Maha smiled, "It is so good to see you once again", and they embraced once more. They stood back at arm's length and looked at one other. Their amethyst eyes connected, communicating unspoken words. Maha then turned to the two who had answered the door. "Namid! Tisane! Oh, my beautiful sisters!" she said, and with that, all four hugged and held each other. Ruby watched as Maha reunited with her loved ones. She felt a little lonely. It was the first time she had not had Maha's full attention and it took some getting used to. They then all turned to Ruby, and within moments Maha reached and pulled her into the small group. "Ruby, these are my beautiful sisters. Tisane here," she looked at her sister, "the untamed wild one, the gypsy of the family" she laughed as Tisane came and hugged Ruby tightly. She was slender with long, flaxen hair and a halo of coloured tiny flowers around her head. She was dressed in a silken robe that was soft aqua-blue in colour.

Ruby watched as Namid came over to hug her. "Hello, I am Namid. My name means star dancer", Namid said matter-of-factly. She was also petite; the smallest of the sisters with the darkest of hair similar to Maha's, adorned with tiny jewels that created a galaxy of stars within her hair. "Welcome to our village and home, Ruby", said Eaven as she came over and gave Ruby a warm hug. "My sister has guided you home." Eaven turned to look at Maha with what looked like, Ruby thought, a sadness in her eyes. They walked over to the corner of the hall to a small table made from a tree stump. It was laden with wonderful treats.

They all sat down around the table on tiny, pillow-like cushions. The bowls and cups were shaped from waxy leaves. Ruby could see blackberries, strawberries, nuts, pine nuts, sunflower seeds, nasturtium petals and fruits of every description. It looked like a table laid for a fairy queen's home coming. Tisane poured Ruby a cup of dark red liquid. "This is bloom berry juice", she said to Ruby. "Delicious!" Ruby responded. She had grown to love bloom berries, and now to drink it was a wonderful experience and treat. The five of them sat and ate, drank and laughed as they all told tales of their adventures. It was a long time later that Ruby realised how tired she was. Namid led her behind the silk curtains. There was a small lantern glowing in the corner. The floor looked like one giant, fluffy silken pillow. The nymphs had laid down a large woven blanket and a pillow for her head to rest upon.

"These fabrics are made by the silkworms and filled with cotton flowers", said Namid smiling. "You will sleep well tonight, Ruby. She hugged Ruby and disappeared behind the curtain into the room. Tisane and Eaven popped their heads through the curtain and said "Goodnight Ruby", and blew her a kiss. Ruby smiled. She felt so full, so warm, and so loved. As the curtain fell back together, she heard Maha say goodnight to her sisters. Ruby looked through the join in the curtain and saw how much love they had for each other. It warmed her heart. Maha let them out of the front door and walked back towards Ruby. "I will say goodnight, my dear friend. I am sure you will sleep the sleep of a thousand dreams tonight. You will be safe, comfortable and warm. My sisters have done well to welcome us". Ruby replied, "I am humbled by their generosity. You are blessed to have such wonderful family with so much love". Maha smiled and nodded. "I am blessed. When we are born, we understand we will one day depart to be a guide for a realm traveler. It has been my family's love and unconditional support that has been in my heart to guide me."

"I will see you tomorrow, dear one. Rest now, and the sweetest of dreams." Maha came over and hugged Ruby. They had formed a deep soul connection that would be forever. Ruby heard Maha close the door behind her, and for the first time, she was alone. Ruby looked around the hall. They had made it so comfy just for her, knowing she was too large for the village homes. She was overwhelmed by these gorgeous little people, and their generosity and kindness. She finally lay amongst the soft cotton filled pillow and silken blankets, and fell into a deep, deep slumber.

CHAPTER FIFTEEN

As the daylight streamed through the small windows above her in the hall, Ruby lay amongst the soft covers, looking up at the thatched roof. She was recalling the night before; Maha and her sisters, the community, and how happy they had been to see her. Maha had told Ruby when they first met that she had been chosen to be Ruby's guide. "Her guide?" Ruby wondered to herself. "She has guided me through so many things already". Their journey together had been one of deep, deep attainment. Was this where she was to be guided to? This quaint village full of gentle happy fae folk. Or were they yet to journey on from here? She would have to see what the days ahead held. She had grown so fond of Maha. Her wonderful company, her wisdom and her gentleness. Yes, she truly valued and respected Maha as her friend.

There was a tiny knock at the door. Ruby got up and opened it. There was Tisane, "gypsy child" and Namid, "star dancer" beaming their bright smiles at her, with their amethyst eyes alight; wide and full of joy. Outside in the street, the sun shone brightly.

Ruby instantly felt the good vibe from them and welcomed them in with a big smile. What a wonderful start to her day. Tisane carried a knapsack on her back made from what looked like a bundle wrapped in beige coloured cloth; similar to Maha's that she had packaged her bloom berries in. This one, however, was a much bigger version, and was tied with a thicker vine. Tisane skipped over to the table they had sat at the night before, and untied the cloth to reveal an instant table cloth. She revealed home cooked pancakes that had been made by the local village baker and hollowed out giant seed pods that held blackcurrant jam and another pod of honey. "From the bees", announced Namid, eagerly sharing this information with Ruby. Ruby sat with Namid and Tisane, and feasted like a queen again on the scrumptious pancakes with honey and jam.

She wondered where Maha and her sister Eaven were, but was so entertained listening to Tisane and her funny stories. She seemed to be the cheeky rebel and Namid with her gentle caring nature, the nurturer of the two. As Tisane spoke of their village and the folk who lived there, she told of tales of the marketplace, the weaver, baker and festivals of bright colours; full of cheer and laughter, flowers and music. Ruby could imagine it all. Eaven appeared at the door just as they were finishing off their morning feast, with a warm bloom berry tea. "Good morning, Ruby", she said brightly as she entered the hall. "I trust you slept well, and my little sisters have been gracious to you this morning", as she looked at Tisane and Namid, smiling. "Good morning, Eaven. Oh, yes, thank you. There is so much food. I can barely move; I am so full." They all laughed. Eaven greeted her sisters with a big embrace and sat down to share a bloom berry tea. She spoke of the village folk who were busy preparing for a celebration. Ruby had heard the noise of hustle and bustle passing her windows in the morning as she had laid in bed. "Maybe it was market day" she wondered.

When they had finished their tea, Eaven asked Ruby to follow her as they left Namid and Tisane behind in the hall. They walked down the side of the hall to a pathway that led away from the village. The sun was shining, and the warmth was already soaking into Ruby's skin. The butterflies were in flight around them; sometimes landing on the pretty wildflowers to drink their nectar. They were walking along a pathway amongst the grasses and trees when they came to a small clearing. It was open to the blue skies but was surrounded by a glade of trees, so the clearing was hidden from the village. There was no one there. The clearing was actually a natural mineral spring. It was a hot spring with water gently rising up and releasing bubbles of steam as they popped on the surface. Ruby watched as the steam rose from the water.

Eaven spoke, "We have brought you here to prepare for the celebration, and to bathe and cleanse". As she spoke, Tisane and Namid appeared from the glade into the clearing, carrying woven baskets and cloths draped over their arms. They smiled at Ruby.

"Take the time you need, and I shall return", Eaven said as she smiled and turned to walk back towards the village. Ruby wanted to call out and ask where Maha was, but she was distracted by Tisane who was giggling, trying to help her remove her wand netting from off her shoulder. Ruby had carried it everywhere. Tisane helped Ruby remove the wand netting and amulet pouch from around her neck. Ruby held on to the pouch and her crystal necklace and said she wanted to keep them on. She had not taken it off since Maha had given her the pouch, and in it contained her crystals of clear quartz, amber, aquamarine and turquoise. She held on to the pouch tightly with her hand. Namid asked for Ruby's cotton night dress and the sisters turned their heads away to give Ruby privacy. As she removed the nightdress she laid it upon the rock and stepped into the springs.

It was glorious! Warm, bubbling water surrounded her body as she sank lower in the water. Ruby lowered herself until the water reached her neck. She held her head backwards to wet her hair and let water cover her face. She held her head up and from behind her felt Namid hold her hair. Namid was sitting on the rock behind Ruby with a small jug and began to scoop water from the springs, pouring it over Ruby's scalp. It felt divine! It was soothing. She let the waters wash over her. Ruby soaked in the springs for some time as Namid explained that they had been chosen to bathe Ruby and prepare her for the celebration. It was a great honour for them. Ruby sat up a little, with her body partly out of the water to allow Namid behind her to wash her hair. Namid used a blend she had made from the oils of rose and honeysuckle. The scent was exquisite; it filled the area with a beautiful floral aroma.

Namid massaged Ruby's hair and rinsed it with the spring water. As Namid washed her hair, Tisane was sitting on the grass area near the springs and began to make a flower chain with daisies she had collected in her basket. She wove them into a vine and made a halo crown. She lovingly added fine silk strands falling from the back of the halo like a waterfall of flowers and silken thread. Ruby was feeling extremely pampered, fresh and clean. She stood to dry off with the cloths that had been laid upon the rock. She noticed Tisane had laid out her cotton nightdress on another rock for her, all freshly washed and had dried in the sun. It felt clean and crisp again. She placed it over her head. Her hair still damp, she shook her hair free and smelt the honeysuckle and rose scent fill the air.

Ruby walked over to Namid and Tisane both sitting in the grass and sat down next to them. She watched as Tisane wove the vines and flowers into a halo. She admired the beautiful work and the fine silken threads falling down. They were so fine and intricate; fit for a Fairy Queen. Tisane had now made two of them, and they were identical. Tisane and Namid were both quiet now and Ruby felt their silence. She wondered where Maha was. "Where is Maha today?" she asked the sisters. The sisters looked at each other; their amethyst eyes connecting as Ruby had seen

before. Ruby marveled at the knowing between them, the connection, the unspoken words. Namid answered. "Maha is with Eaven, preparing for the celebration also. They have much to do and say. They will be with us soon enough", she replied, smiling slightly at Ruby. Ruby was left feeling a little unsure. The sisters had seemed to lose their bright spark. Their happiness was there, but fading.
Her intuition told her that there was more to Namid's answer. They looked saddened; especially compared to last night.

As they sat in a group in the sun, Ruby's hair had dried now and Namid had begun to comb and braid Ruby's long golden hair. She pulled Ruby's hair back from her face and on either side, began to plait intricate braids. She tied them off with a fine vine. As Namid braided, Tisane now finished with her halos and had begun to decorate Ruby's hair with white flowers from her basket; creamy white gardenias. Their scent was heavenly. Tiny white daisies, divinely scented jasmine, and a small green leaf ivy vine was woven through the braid. Ruby put her hand up to her braids and felt them tightly woven. She breathed in the scent of honeysuckle and rose, and the gardenia and jasmine flowers in her hair.
She felt so clean and pretty. Her white cotton nightdress was so white and fresh, and her hair reminded her of a goddess.

Tisane put the two halos into her basket, and the three of them began to walk back along the path to the village. They reached a fork in the path; one pathway led to the village, and the other in a direction of the hill behind. Namid asked Ruby to follow her. Tisane hugged her sister and Ruby and said she would join them soon. Tisane took the pathway to the village. Namid and Ruby took the path to the hill. Ruby followed Namid, 'star dancer'. She was so petite and delicate; smaller than Maha. She had the same dark silken hair as Maha too, only sprinkled with jewels that glistened amongst her hair. She was gliding along barely touching the earth, just like Maha. She looked so light; it was as if she would float off at any moment. They followed the path away from the village, up upon a grassy open hill. It was not a large mountain peak like she had scaled before; just a small grassy hill.

Ruby was being led far away from the village and could not see the outskirts as she looked back. She could barely make out the springs where she had bathed this morning. "Namid, please stop", Ruby called out. "Please tell me where we are going. I feel I need to see Maha." Namid turned around and with a sadness in her amethyst pools of eyes, replied, "Do not worry, sweet one. We will be seeing Maha soon". They continued for a short time - the sun now ending its day - the sky colours of pinks, reds and oranges as it slowly sank into another night's deep slumber. The moon began to rise into the clear sky above. "Not many stars out tonight", thought Ruby. It was a very clear sky, and a magnificent dusk.

CHAPTER SIXTEEN

As they neared the top of the hill, the sun was now in slumber as the moon was rising, providing the light they needed. Ruby noticed a perfectly formed circle, with massive jagged topped pillars of stone. There were gaps between each pillar, like makeshift doorways in and out of the circle. She walked to the crest; the top of the hill. The moon was now gaining power upon the sun and up it rose slowly, increasing in size as the night sky became darker. As Namid and Ruby approached the outside of this massive circle, Namid stopped outside of the largest stone. She did not enter the circle. Ruby watched as Namid looked down the hill in the direction from which they had come. From far below, Ruby could see a trail of lights weaving their way up the hill, snaking in a long line. Slowly and surely, the lights became bigger and brighter as she noticed the villagers all making their way up to the crest of the hill where they both waited.

Ruby watched as the procession approached. As they reached the crest of the hill, they were in a long line of two, side by side. The first two villagers bowed to Ruby as they neared her and then parted; one taking the direction to the left, and one taking to the right, taking place around the outside of the circle stones. As the line of villagers made their way up the hill, this continued; them all bowing and separating from their line until there were only a few villagers left. It was then that Ruby saw Tisane with her basket, and Eaven side by side, carrying their lanterns. They bowed to Ruby and parted to take place either side of Namid. Ruby looked behind them and her breath was taken away by the exquisite beauty before her. Maha, the last in the procession, was not carrying a lantern; she did not need to. Her beauty could light the night's sky. She was dressed in a white silken robe and her beautiful dark hair, which was usually long and free, was braided with white flowers and vines the same as Ruby's. She stood in front of Ruby and they embraced. It was a long embrace.

As they parted, Ruby felt happy to see Maha but knew this was something so big - larger than her - larger than them. She looked at Maha for reassurance. Maha turned to Namid and held her sister. She kissed both cheeks and looked into her eyes. There again, Ruby noticed that same look - the amethyst connection - no words were spoken. Maha moved across to Eaven and repeated this ritual. She held her gaze with Eaven for a long time, and finally to Tisane. After this had occurred, Tisane knelt to her basket and pulled from it the two beautiful halos she had created earlier on the grass. Tisane passed the halos to Eaven who gently placed one upon

Maha's head and the other on Ruby's. She bowed and the three sisters took their place around the outer circle. Maha looked at Ruby and took her hand to lead Ruby into the circle. The full moon was high now. Its light shone into the centre circle, creating a theatrical feel.

Ruby took a glance back at the darkness and the tiny lights of the village. She looked around the outer circle to see all the village folk decorated with flowers in their hair and lanterns held. Ruby swore she saw tears, or was it all those amethyst pools of eyes glistening at her in the moonlight? Ruby reached for assurance and held Maha's hand. Maha held her hand up to Ruby as if to gently say, "Stop, it is okay", and she released Ruby's hand and entered the circle alone. Her white silken gown slowly caught the gentle night breeze, and her hair glistened with jewels and flowers. Maha held her arms up high into the air, with her back towards Ruby, and began to speak out loud to the Moon.

"Divine Mother,
She who is life, she who is love,
Appear to me now,
To complete my quest, to complete the cycle.
Your wisdom and sacred energy we honour.
Divine Mother,
She who is life, she who is love."

Maha repeated this several times with her arms held high. The villagers around the circle outside the stones began to slowly hum with the angelic tone Ruby had heard once before, but this time it was gentle and continual; filling the air with music. Ruby had tingles up and down her spine. She could feel the angelic call. She felt the connecting energy and could see light beginning to grow in the centre of the circle. Maha was calling upon the Goddess.

Eaven stood beside Ruby humming and watching Maha. She was also tranced, as were the other nymphs all calling as one. A collective energy surged around the circle. As Maha called to the night sky, she fell to her knees. She had released; she had weakened. The light was now very bright around her. Ruby watched as Maha buckled to the earth. Ruby wanted to run in and help her, but as she began to move, a beautiful vision - a woman, a Goddess - appeared before her in the circle. She had appeared from a mirage of golden light. She *was* the light.

Her golden gown, long, flowing flaxen hair, and her soft, draping golden sleeves fell to the earth in flowing points. She leant forward to give her hand to Maha. She gently beckoned Maha to stand. Maha stood in front of this ethereal vision; the Goddess. She was in awe of the sight before her. Maha looked back at Ruby; her eyes now illuminated with bright, white light. Ruby entered the circle. She walked slowly towards Maha and the ethereal being in front of them. As she entered from the darkness of the outside circle, the golden light became so bright, it was lighting up the inner circle; a golden purity emanating from the Goddess. They stood side by side, and Maha and Ruby were mesmerised by the light.

"I am Nitesh, Goddess and Keeper of the Earth. You have called upon me and I have answered your call. I am here to complete the cycle; to complete the spiral of life, and to heal past, present and future", the Goddess spoke. Maha turned to face Ruby and held both of Ruby's hands in front of Nitesh. As they faced each other, Ruby could faintly hear the sweet angelic music from the nymphs floating around the skies; the harmony and tone spiraling gently around the inner circle, blending with the golden light. Glistening like particles floated in the night air.

Maha began to speak as she held Ruby's hands in hers. "From birth, I have known that my tribe, my people born of this realm, all know we are born to serve; to guide one home. We have a connection - a deep soul connection - that has spanned realms for as long as time. We will meet again. And again, we will look different, and feel different, but when we meet, we will know. Our souls will know. They will connect and we will once again love, protect and guide each other. I will look for you again in the next, and the next." Ruby was welling up with tears and emotion. She could hardly see in front of her. "It can't be, it can't be", she thought. It sounded like a goodbye. This can't be. Her friend, her beautiful soul friend saying goodbye? Her heart was slowly shattering. Maha continued holding Ruby's hands tightly. "You have journeyed your quest, and I have journeyed mine in this realm. I have served and guided to lead you to here. We have sought answers through FIRE, WATER, AIR and now EARTH. With that, I give you my final gift. She reached into her amulet pouch and passed Ruby a dark black smooth stone. "It is Onyx, Ruby, your final piece of elemental crystal. This will protect you and keep you grounded. Always trust in your intuition."

As Ruby took the gift, she looked into Maha's eyes, hoping this was not so, but Maha's eyes did not lie - they told truth - she *was* truth. Her amethyst eyes began to pool with tears. As they connected, Ruby knew this must be. She knew Maha was born for this very moment; to have her guide her soul connection through the elementals to journey, to learn, to grow, so Ruby may take these lessons forward into the next realm. Ruby broke eye contact and began to realize the gravity of the situation; unaware of the increasing vibrational sounds coming from the outside of the circle, and unaware of this magnificent Goddess before them. She began to cry, and felt silent tears streaming down her face. She looked around to see if she could run and drag Maha to escape; to turn back time. But time was *now* and it had all been leading to this moment. She felt as if her heart was breaking into tiny pieces. Ruby felt ill and began to feel dizzy.

Maha leant forward to steady her and asked Ruby for her amulet pouch. Ruby took if from around her neck and gave it to Maha. Maha opened it and passed the crystals of the Elementals to Nitesh. Ruby watched Nitesh slowly place each crystal into a chalice-like goblet etched with symbols and spirals. As she spoke out, she looked up so the Universe could see and hear. She held each crystal up into to the night; the moon as a witness.

*"I call upon Amber from the Guardians of FIRE, from the South,
Aquamarine from the Guardians of Water from the West,
Turquoise from the Guardians of AIR from the East,
Onyx from the Guardians of Earth from the North..."*

and finally, she placed all the crystals in the chalice and added in the clear quartz crystal.

"Here, I place quartz crystal; the essence of life from SPIRIT."

She held the chalice high above her head; to the moon, to the sky, and to the Earth.

"I call upon the Elementals; the Guardians, the Keepers of these realms. Take these gifts to allow constellations of truth to reside within you, to bring you peaceful feelings of oneness, and with every atom of your being, live your truth, with purity of heart and love. Take these gifts and allow their powers and lessons to merge into pure light to lead you from times of darkness. Wisdom, love and peace be with you. We are all children of the universe and there we shall return. There, you will find your divine purpose."

Maha looked at Ruby and asked for the Ash wand. Ruby, with tears streaming down her face, was still holding Maha's tiny delicate hand in hers. She did not want to let go as she reached over and untied the netting that held her wand. She passed it to Maha. Maha delivered it to Nitesh. As Nitesh lowered her arms holding the chalice, she walked with it into the direct centre of the circle and placed the chalice down upon the earth. She held the ash wand in her hand and with one complete turn of her body sent her robes billowing into the air. The golden light emanating from her now was growing brighter. The tone of the outside of the circle began to pick up volume and harmony; much higher and louder than before. As Nitesh spun, the ground beneath her began to light up, and before them appeared a glowing labyrinth. Ruby became frightened. With the tone gaining in volume and the labyrinth growing in size, the light from the centre was no longer a golden body, but a glowing orb of pure light.

Ruby held Maha's hand. She was afraid. She was not prepared, and she was not ready. "Ready for what?" she cried. The fear of losing her friend was so strong. The vibration created a humming within the inner circle, and the labyrinth was pulsing with light. Nitesh was nowhere to be seen, but just the glowing orb and the chalice upon the earth in the centre.

Maha turned to Ruby. "It is time, dear one", she said. "No!" cried Ruby, holding Maha's arm with both hands. "Please don't leave me!

Don't go!" she begged. Maha faced Ruby and gently released Ruby's grip upon her arm. She settled her with those gorgeous amethyst eyes. The vibration was now deeper. The humming and light whirled in front of them in the centre of the labyrinth.

"Ruby, it is my time. My quest here is done. We shall meet again in another realm, another time. We shall never forget this connection. It is imprinted in our souls." Maha looked back to her sisters, and they bowed to her with respect and love of this beautiful woman. Maha kissed Ruby's forehead. "Till next time, beautiful one" she said as she looked upon Ruby one last time with her beautiful amethyst eyes. She turned around and began to enter the glowing labyrinth. Ruby watched her body rigid as Maha slowly walked to the centre; the vibrational pitch heightening as Maha neared the centre orb of light. The labyrinth began to pulse and glow, the closer Maha got. As she entered the centre, Maha leant down to pick up the Chalice and put it to her lips. She drank from it and returned it to the earth.

As she turned around, she looked back at Ruby. Ruby was feeling dizzy and overwhelmed by the sights and sounds. She watched as her beautiful Maha, surrounded by the golden radiance, held up her right hand to Ruby as if to say that final goodbye. What Maha was revealing was a beautiful glowing spiral design on her hand. Ruby looked down to her hand and then held hers up to mirror Maha. Her spiral design was beginning to glow. Ruby finally understood. She was witnessing the spiral of life; past present and future. She looked up once more to connect with Maha; her eyes burning with tears. She was forever grateful for this beautiful being that had guided her and protected her through her lessons. She held her hand up high to Maha for the last time in eternal gratitude. The vibration intensified as Nitesh appeared from within the centre orb like a beam of golden power, and held her hands high. Ruby turned to see Maha walk into the golden light, and within a split second, the orb became a majestic power of pure white light energy. Nitesh, still spinning, gathered the orb of energy - Maha's beautiful pure white light energy - and with both hands, guided the energy towards the night sky, into the heavens.

"Oh, beautiful Maha", Ruby wept out loud, as she watched the white light energy rise high above into the night skies, spreading itself amongst the stars. Maha, beautiful Child of the Earth. Ruby turned, her heart breaking, and tears flowing down her cheek. She began to slowly walk towards the entrance of the Labyrinth. The intensity as she entered inside the labyrinth was so much stronger. The golden light emanated from the centre guiding her in. The centre glowed brighter now; she could not see Nitesh, Goddess of the Earth; just a spiraling golden light. Ruby could hear the vibrations from the outside of the labyrinth, but inside as she walked and turned, and walked another corner, she felt the humming gain strength and the light becoming brighter. It was a surreal feeling.

Ruby walked towards the energy pull of the centre, towards the light. A new realm; a new beginning now, to take with her the knowledge she had learnt in this realm and empowerments from the Goddess; to teach, to heal and love as a chosen one. She held her head high as she came to the centre. She could see the chalice glowing from the light surrounding it. Ruby could feel the energy spinning around her; enveloping her in its warm glow. She had come full circle. She was closing the circle. Ruby leant down to pick up the chalice and drank from it.

"Fire, Water, Air, Earth and Spirit within", she chanted. She held her hands up to the spiraling centre of the circle, and looked up to Maha; sparkling in the heavens. Ruby felt the power surging through her; the power of the elementals. She felt Mother Earth below her, and she became one with the power. As the vibrations heightened, she looked to the sky one last time while the white light orb spun and closed around her. Ruby held her hands high, reaching for the heavens above, as the energy pulsing around her drew her in. Earth and sky connected. The elementals had joined. She was a child of the universe. The ground began to fall below her. Ruby began to spiral down into the memories of her mind. Down, down she spiraled; twisting and turning, white light flashing, and memories of her journey sinking into her soul; for it was her soul that would recall them. "Fire, Water, Air, Earth, and Spirit, return me home", she chanted. Ruby was spiraling through the dimensions of time, until she lost control of her thoughts. The light and vibrations enveloped her and she lost consciousness.

Pink and lemon hues coloured the early morning skies. The dewy grass and birdsong was heralding in a new day. Ruby woke upon the dampened grass. She looked up into the tinted sky and felt the coolness below her. Sitting up, she grabbed her unruly auburn hair and swept it to one side. It did not want to stay there. She tried tucking it behind her ears, but it seemed to have a mind of its own. She twisted to look behind her. The ancient Tor with its first rays of sunshine shone upon the ancient monument. Dawn had broken. Ruby rubbed her eyes and realised she was in her cotton nightdress. "Oh my goodness, how long have I been asleep here?" she wondered out loud as she tried to recall last night's steps. She did recall walking up to the Tor drawn by the brilliant moon, which was barely visible in the morning sky.

"I must have fallen asleep", she thought, as she was suddenly shocked into action. "The bus!" she remembered. Ruby sprung to her feet and wondered what time it was as she descended the many steps of the hilltop. As she reached the crest of the hill, she took a last look back at the majestic Tor;

imagining it to be so full of secrets and stories. She wished she had more time to explore. She felt so alive as she was looking down at the village below beginning to stir. Ruby managed to reach the cottage without anyone seeing her in her nightdress. "What on earth was I doing asleep on the grass?" she chuckled to herself. "Another one for the book!" she thought.

Ruby entered the cottage quietly, and went straight to the bathroom to shower. After a nice hot shower, she was in her bedroom changing and looked out of her cottage window. "One last time", she told herself. She drew open the curtain and looked out the window. The vision was etched in her memory; a memory of the moonlit night she had felt the Tor drawing her there. A memory that would never leave her. As she closed the cottage door - backpack on - she made her way along the cobbled road to the town. She wondered where her adventures would take her now. The bus driver stood in the town centre as promised, waving his arms. "Good morning, young lady. Jump on in! We have to get you to your destination" he said, cheerfully. He looked so much chirpier than the night before, when they had left him standing in the rain.

Ruby looked up to the bus window. It still had the same blue velour seats she could see. She turned to the driver standing at the door and then turned to the road leading away from town. As she looked ahead, she hesitated for a moment and turned back to the driver.

"Thanks very much", she replied, "but I think I will be okay". She waved goodbye to the bus driver and began walking out of the town until she found the main motorway.

Loving the wind in her hair, she had decided it could fly as free as it liked; she didn't try to tame it. Ruby felt wonderful; as free as a bird, and felt such a sense of peace as she walked. The day was blessed with blue skies and scattered fluffy white clouds as she looked into the sky. Loving the sense of freedom in her step, she felt alive; strong and full of unknown excitement. She was walking for some time, when an old camper van pulled up just in front of her on the gravel. The driver; a dark haired young man, leant over and unwound the passenger window. "Hi there, need a ride?" he asked. She reflected for a moment as she glanced ahead at the road. "Yeah, why not", she said as she opened the door. Ruby pushed her pack into the camper van, pulled herself up into the seat and sat down.

"Where are you heading?" he asked. He smiled and leant in front of her to wind the window back up. As he did, he revealed a spiral tattoo on his hand. Ruby felt herself go faint as if she had fallen instantly into a void in time. Deja vu? She looked down at her own hand and saw the same spiral marking. She looked across to him and then ahead into the distance as far as her eyes could see. Smiling, she turned to him as he started the ignition and said, "Where am I heading, you ask? On a Journey".

About the Author

Nicola C. Stokes was born in Nottingham U.K and now lives with her husband and son in Melbourne, Australia. She is a certified SoulCollage® facilitator and currently studying Holistic Counselling and Flower Essence Therapy. Nicola's inspiration comes from her passion of travel, crystals, mystical elementals, creative pursuits and personal development. She is constantly evolving and learning through lessons and blessings on her life's journey.

My story begins in Glastonbury, a small market town considered to be the spiritual, holy sacred centre of England. The town is known for many reasons and visited as a sacred centre and pilgrimage for visitors all over the world.

Glastonbury Tor is a majestic conical hill with the 14th century, 520ft ancient tower of St. Michael sitting upon its grassy summit; a beacon that can be seen for miles around, rising above the inland sea, once fabled to be Isle of Avalon with its swirling mists and mystical lands. Some believe the seven level sculptured terraces that lead to the summit are a physical and metaphysical journey within. Others believe these were built as a processional pathway by the monks, some as a mystical maze or labyrinth to worship Mother Earth; a place of Goddess worship.

Ancient fables tell that Glastonbury is the resting place of King Arthur and his bride Queen Guinevere; so, steeped in mystery and magic. It was a place where Priestesses' of Avalon and druids following the Goddess could worship alongside Christian Monks. Jesus's uncle, Joseph of Arimathea was said to have made several journeys to Glastonbury, and returned as a Christian missionary with a party of twelve monks to Wearay Hill. He was believed to have struck his staff into the ground, and from where it struck, miraculously grew and burst into leaf. This Hawthorn tree that flowers every Easter still stands and is known as The Glastonbury Thorn.

The Chalice Well at the base of the Tor is an ancient well with continual Red flowing spring water, fed by the Red spring from under Chalice Hill. Close by is the White spring, which is fed from deep under the Tor. Travelers come from far and wide to visit the Chalice Well to see the heavy oak and wrought iron well cover, with the Vesica Piscis crossed with the symbol of a sword to represent King Arthur's Excalibur. They come to drink the water from both the Red and White springs, which are said to contain healing properties.

Fact or fiction; it is up to you to decide, but one thing for certain is that Glastonbury - with its ancient history, spiritual feel, and wisdom - allows the traveller to explore and connect deep within. There is a magical feel within this ancient town where the legends and myths come alive and allow new pilgrims to awaken.

www.ingramcontent.com/pod-product-compliance
Lightning Source LLC
Chambersburg PA
CBHW071006120726
47910CB00004B/1410